Praise for Ann Cory's Melting Iron

"...Ann Cory gives us an astonishingly heartwarming story of love found in the face of a terrifying historical event. I recommend this one." ~ *Euro Reviews*

"...If you enjoy a story with a wealth of sexual tension, then Melting Iron is a necessary read. An intriguing story, rich with suspense and expectation." ~ *Just Erotic Romance Reviews*

Ann Cory

Ann Cory's passion has always been writing thanks to a relentless muse and an overactive imagination. Her biggest fans and supporters include her adorable son, handsome husband, and two crazy cats.

Erotic romance author Ann Cory invites you to sample her literary offerings in the hopes of leaving you with an acquired taste for sophisticated reading. Visit her website http://www.anncory.com or blog http://anncory.blogspot.com/ to see what is new on her publication menu, or join either her no-chat newsletter group http://groups.yahoo.com/group/anncorypostcards or her more social group http://groups.yahoo.com/group/anncory.

Melting Iron

Ann Cory

A SAMHAIN PUBLISHING, LTD. publisher.

Samhain Publishing, Ltd.
2932 Ross Clark Circle, #384
Dothan, AL 36301
www.samhainpublishing.com

Melting Iron
Copyright © 2006 by Ann Cory
Print ISBN: 1-59998-272-2
Digital ISBN: 1-59998-064-9

Editing by Jessica Bimberg
Cover by Scott Carpenter

First Samhain Publishing, Ltd. electronic publication: July 2006
First Samhain Publishing, Ltd. print publication: October 2006

Dedication

For my mother, a woman of incredible strength and beauty. I love you and miss you very much.

Chapter One

The softness of his hands surprised her. Each touch radiated enough heat to melt the coldness from around her heart. She couldn't remember it ever being this way. No man, not even her husband, had ever caressed her flesh with such intended passion.

"You want me, don't you?"

She stared at his mouth. Firm, full, supple lips. They breathed new life into her with each fervent kiss. Was it wrong to want another man when she was married? Instincts told her the answer was clear. She was an adult, not a child. Of course it was wrong. It was a sin in the eyes of the church, though she never attended. Her faith was spiritual, inspired by nature and the world around her. She was a peace-loving woman. When there was a balance with the world around her, Evelynn felt balanced.

Still, the word infidelity played at her. It sparked mixed emotions, almost like a dare. It was forbidden. Disrespectful even. Why would she consider it?

He was excruciatingly close, making her body ache. His brows furrowed as he watched her. Full of curiosity and deep thought.

"What stops you from saying yes?"

His question was a double-edged sword. He knew, as well as she did, what the consequences were. Why was he baiting her? Evelynn shook her head. No. The question was why was she letting him?

As if in answer she held out her hand, her fingers pointing downward. The dim light of the lantern brought out the fine lines across her skin. She was nearly twenty-eight but her hands showed signs of aging. The silver band around her finger didn't reflect the light; instead it appeared dull and faded. She sighed. The ring reminded her of the relationship with her husband.

He jutted out his chin and looked hard into her eyes. "I am well aware of the piece of jewelry branded around your finger. Tell me, because I'm eager to hear, what does the ring signify for you?"

Evelynn parted her lips to speak, but nothing came out. She wasn't ready for serious questions. Whenever he was near, her mind shut off. All logical thoughts vanished. He was patient, though, and would wait for some kind of comment before continuing on with his line of questioning. With a dismissive shrug, she glanced off to the far corner of the barn.

"It means I have someone to answer to." She looked back at him, their eyes locked in a challenging gaze. Her heart swelled and pounded fiercely. She forced herself to swallow to keep her heart in place.

"And do you answer to him?"

Evelynn narrowed her eyes. "Not in the way you are suggesting."

His brows arched and he crossed his arms. "No? Please. Enlighten me."

Every nerve in her body was on edge.

She fixed her fists on her hips and tried to summon up a little attitude.

"What I mean is, I don't do whatever he commands. I am my own person, and I intend to remain unchanged. He may have given me a ring and a new last name, but he hasn't stripped me of my identity."

There. She'd said the words. The problem was they weren't at all true. She hoped by saying them enough, eventually she would believe it. Evelynn had very little idea of who she was anymore, and it terrified her about as much as being alone in the same room with the young man she secretly fancied.

"No man ever should take away your identity."

Her body shook as she realized how close he now stood. "Wh-what?"

"No man should ever make a woman change or take away her self-worth."

Evelynn snorted. He was just a young man, what did he know? "It's not as simple as you make it out to be. When two people live under the same roof for a long time, under the binding laws of marriage, they change. You give up certain things for one another."

"I see. In other words they strike a compromise. They find ways to be equals in the household. Am I getting warmer?"

She bit her lip. His presence warmed her entire being. Damn him and his desirable body. She wanted to attack him and pummel him with kisses everywhere. The explicit thought surprised her, but the desire did not. Her dreams were always very real.

There was no way she was going to win here. Not with him less than a foot away, spouting the ideas of what marriage should be like, knowing full well they weren't the same as her ideals. Her tight fists strained her wrists.

"I don't want to talk about this anymore. Anything I say you are going to find something to argue about. I should go."

He reached out, catching a tuft of fabric from her dress. "I'm not trying to argue with you. I only want to understand. I had hoped you would stay a while longer."

His smile made it clear he would do whatever it took to sway her decision. He moved toward her, closing the distance to the point she could smell the soot in his hair. A manly scent she had grown to adore rather than turn away from. Her heart thudded and she was certain he could hear it.

"You and I hold a lot of the same beliefs. In my mind, marriage means different things for each and every person. Both men and women." He paused and stood before her, the tips of his boots touching her bare toes.

"When I look into your beautiful blue eyes, I see a tremendous amount of sadness. It will destroy you, if it hasn't all ready. I see a precious life not being lived to its fullest. You, my dear sweet Evelynn, aren't some item to be used and discarded on a daily basis. In the time I've lived here, I have never seen your husband look at you with the same kind of excitement I feel coursing through my veins. I've never even witnessed him touch you with a gentle hand."

She puffed out her chest and put her hands on her hips. "And I suppose you can see through walls?"

He pressed his finger to her lips and shook his head. The feel of his skin sent her mind into a flurry of confusion.

"It breaks my heart to think you have resigned yourself to this dismal way of life. There is a burst of energy inside you waiting to get out. I can see it!"

She laughed nervously and wanted to turn away, but he wouldn't let her gaze falter.

"You deserve to be loved. I want you to know how it feels to have someone think about you from the moment they wake, until the time they fall asleep, and for every second in between. Let me find a way to put hope into your heart and fire in your belly."

Shivers crept along her skin as his lips sought out the curvature of her neck—the sweet spot—where the blend of pleasurable and painful tickles drew the very warmth from between her thighs.

His hands found the clasp of her dress and before she knew it the same supple lips were danced across her breasts, bringing her nipples to life. Her entire being awakened. He cleared away the once hidden shadows and dusted away her anxiety. In slow, controlled movements, he tapped right into the beginnings of heat in her belly, and she welcomed its forbidden flames. Her fingers traipsed through the unruly strands of his hair as she arched her back, pressing her breasts further into him. She closed her eyes while the burning sensations became overwhelming.

He watched her. "Would you deny these very things? Can you honestly say you don't want me?"

A tear fell from her eye, carelessly gliding down her flushed cheek. Her lower lip trembled. Where was her voice when she needed it most?

Daniel's lips brushed against her earlobe, his voice deep and sensuous. "Tell me. I need to hear the words from you. If you want me to leave you alone from now on, I will. But I have to hear it."

His hands lovingly stroked her breasts, circling her nipples with the faintest touch of his fingertips.

"I do want you. I've wanted you from the moment you walked through our door. I have always wanted to know what it felt like to be safe inside your arms."

He smiled and bowed his head, resuming the evocative suckling of her nipples, swathing her ample breasts in his coal-smudged hands. Tonight, for the first time in a long time, she felt like a woman. A woman in love. She wanted it to last forever.

"You have made me very happy. I intend to do the same for you."

Along her thigh she felt the bulge of his erection, prodding at her from beneath his thick trousers. How many nights had she dreamed about him thrusting inside her? How many pairs of undergarments had she soaked when she dreamt about him having his way with her? Countless. And now she'd finally put to rest all the fantasies and make it a reality.

He gently tugged at her dress. "Mind if I help you take this off?"

She shook her head and raised her arms in the air. The cloth of her dress brushed along her nose as he helped remove it, shutting out almost all of the sound inside the barn. All except one.

A slow, distracting thump played in the distance and continued to grow louder until the noise became deafening, shaking the entire foundation of the barn. She tried to grab his body for balance, but he was no longer there. In fact, nothing was there at all, only an empty void. She struggled to grab hold of anything, but it was too late. Down she fell, into the beckoning black pit.

Evelynn opened her eyes and sat up, clutching the sheets of her bed. The collar of her nightgown was soaked from sweat and clung to her neck uncomfortably. She opened her fists, surprised at how much they ached. A gruff voice jolted her out of her bewildered thoughts.

"Sorry. I tried to be quiet walking up the stairs. Go back to sleep."

It was several minutes before her eyes adjusted to the cold pit of darkness. In silence she watched Brandt remove his work shirt and pants and let them fall in a heap to the floor. Once her breathing returned to normal, she lay back.

Her heart thudded in her chest. It had only been a dream. The kind she wished more than anything would come true. A sudden pang of guilt pushed away the images of seduction. She was a married woman and shouldn't be thinking of the embrace of any man except her husband. Though she couldn't remember the last time she had nestled in close to his body.

Without even a leisurely kiss to her damp forehead, her husband climbed into bed and turned away from her, bunching the blankets over his broad, muscular shoulders. Almost instantly he was asleep and snoring quietly.

She stared out the window and looked out at the moon. The lady who lay there knew her deepest, darkest secrets. Evelynn wondered what Daniel was thinking. Did he dream about her as well? Was he even aware what visuals crept in her mind whenever she thought about him?

Sleep would come again but it wouldn't be the same. The stranger lying next to her didn't know anything about what she needed. As a wife. As a person. As a woman. She closed her eyes and waited for the morning light to come. At least in her dreams she was wanted.

Chapter Two

Evelynn watched helplessly as Bess scrubbed away the thick layer of soot along the entryway with a gnarled sponge. She'd reminded her husband time and time again to remove his soiled boots before entering the house, but he never listened. The soles attracted every piece of soil and stray leaves on his walk home.

"It's what we pay the hired help for," he'd always say in his gruff tone. The tone which meant he was the boss and could do as he pleased and damn what anyone else thought. She wondered if he intended for her to feel insignificant or if it were a role she'd become accustomed to. At any rate, she wasn't treated much better than the hired help, and she still couldn't bring herself to do anything about it.

Evelynn was certain her husband resented her for not attending to the house, as any good wife should, but after a time she stopped concerning herself with it. A good wife, in his eyes, wouldn't care about anything but catering to her husband's needs, and she had long since stopped caring about what Brandt wanted. He made enough money to hire someone and she was free to do what she wanted. Though she never felt free.

Over the years, Brandt had become a man she didn't understand and, only recently, despised. She used to try and analyze everything to death, but all it got her were headaches and more disappointment. Her mother had begged her to marry someone who was well-to-do in the community and could offer her things she'd been denied growing up in a poor farming family. She never felt poor, even when children had teased her. The amount of love and support she received from her family was worth more to her than a single cent. Out of love and respect of her mother, she considered the offer from Brandt to marry, being aware a blacksmith was as high as she could go. Being the richest occupation in town, it offered a grand house, servants, and money to afford fancy dresses and shoes.

Evelynn questioned the need for all the grandeur and wasn't impressed with being spoiled, but she wasn't one to work fields or plows either. Growing up with little means to afford more than a few dresses, she spent the bulk of her time daydreaming about a man who would sweep her off her feet and love her like no other. She wasn't ready to marry but neither did she want to attend to her seven other siblings all day. Something had to change.

One day she hoped it would become clear what she was meant to do and what she could offer to the world. For now her days were a void, spirals of darkness that offered her no answers or comfort. If she'd known how unfulfilling her life married to a blacksmith would be, she would have stayed and worked the fields. It had to be better.

When her husband was working, she often spent her time sitting on the veranda, overlooking their extravagant flowerbeds, fantasizing about a different life. Love and communication were lacking in her marriage, and they were both to blame for the breakdown. Brandt meant well, or at least she believed he did. He was a good provider, and certainly worked hard, but he lacked the qualities she admired most in men.

"Ma'am, I'm done with the floors. What would you have me tend to next?"

Evelynn turned and smiled at Bess. The young, portly woman was a true vision, even covered in soot and floor polish. Her chocolate-colored skin was smooth and flawless, her hair as black as a moonless night all wrapped up in a handkerchief. While Brandt called her the maid, she looked at Bess as more of a confidant. A woman she could confide in from time to time instead of talking out loud to herself. She never had a real friend and wanted one desperately. Anyone to replace the void in her lonely existence.

"My dear Bess. I'd say you have more than earned your keep today. Why don't you take a rest until suppertime?"

The maid's eyes grew wide, almost fearful. Big brown orbs surrounded by a flash of white. "But ma'am, the master insisted I don't take breaks. Says I'm not paid for such luxuries."

Blood boiled beneath Evelynn's skin. She let out a long, frustrated sigh and cocked her head to the side. "There is no master in this house. There never was. Brandt can give himself any title he wishes, but I do not live my life based on those titles, and I don't wish for you to either. While my pigheaded husband is at work, you can take orders from me. Or at least, take friendly requests from me. And right now I request for you to take a break."

Bess gathered up her dress and apron, and hustled out of the room, her eyes wild with intrigue and concern.

Evelynn laughed to herself and sat in her comfortable rocking chair. She took out the fan from her pocket and opened it, swaying it to and fro several inches from her face.

Master. Even the word sounded foreign and ridiculous to her. Brandt was certainly not *her* master. It bothered her enough that he made his apprentice call him as such when he was having issues with his overblown ego. There were times she'd overheard their heated conversations and had to escape somewhere. She nearly flinched at the "yes, master" and "no, master" responses and was frightened by the intensity of her husband's harsh tone when he wasn't addressed correctly. There was no reason he had to instill fear into everyone he came into contact with.

Evelynn often believed she was meant to live in a different time, though it wasn't something she could pinpoint. She was certain there were bigger things out there for her, but she was at a loss how to achieve them.

The rigid ways of the townspeople never sat right with her. Rules changed from day to day. People were judged by their money, name, and status in life. As far as she was concerned, a woman had the same intelligence as a man, if not more. In fact, if she were allowed to work outside the home she was sure she'd be a success. Brandt would never allow it, though. Not with his severe ways and oppressive traditions. No wife of his, of the town's only blacksmith no less, would dare humiliate him by raising her voice to him in public or challenge the manner of things.

With eyes closed, Evelynn leaned her head against the back of the chair to give her tense neck a break. She was always tired and unmotivated right before summer. It was nearing the end of May and she longed for the warmer season. Summer brought its own beauty and a buzz of energy with it. She couldn't remember the last time she'd felt completely rested.

She laid her hands in her lap and let out a deep sigh. The leisurely rocking of the chair was calming and helped her drift off into another place. One where a man courted her, kissed her dewy skin, and made her feel on top of the world.

Chapter Three

Delicious aromas of fresh baked biscuits and homemade stew slowly brought Evelynn back to consciousness. She'd napped far too long, though she wasn't sorry for the pleasant dreams that had found her in sleep. It was painfully obvious by the wanting between her thighs how much Daniel had been the subject of her imaginings again. She could almost sink back into the heated moment where his fingers fluttered across her stomach, his body over hers. His lips were always ready to drink from hers.

The intensity of her dreams almost shocked her awake every time. She wasn't the same woman when she dreamt of Daniel. No, instead she was full of longing. There was no boundary to how far she was willing to go. She ached to be taken with a mix of sheer force and unimaginable gentleness at the same time. Was there even such a thing? Each sensuous vision brought her close to the edge. She feared waking to a thunderous orgasm and uttering Daniel's name from her breathless voice.

A clatter of dishes echoing from the spacious kitchen quickly alerted her to consciousness and got her to her feet.

"Bess, please tell me you did something for yourself while I was asleep. I meant it when I said for you to take a break. You work much too hard around here to not take time out and enjoy yourself."

The maid nodded but refused to look her in the eye. "I did, ma'am. I rested a bit."

Evelynn crossed her arms and tapped her foot. "But not for long, now did you?"

"No, and I am sorry, ma'am. I wanted to do what you said, more than anything, but I was overcome with guilt. What if the master had come home early and seen me resting? I'd surely be whipped or sent away. I need this job. I'd never hear the end of it from my mama."

Her heart went out to the young woman. "Oh, Bess, I am not angry with you in the slightest. My only hope was for you to take time out for yourself rather than spend every minute cleaning one mess or another. We must have the most spotless home of anyone I know."

"Thank you, ma'am."

"I hate how my husband has instilled such a ridiculous amount of fear in you. It is unwarranted. He may bark, but he has little to no bite, I assure you. I would never allow him to dismiss you from here, especially since I consider you a friend. He may think he runs this household with an iron-clad fist, but I most certainly make it my place to have the final say."

"Yes, ma'am. He is a strong man, your husband."

Evelynn sighed. "Oh, Bess, I do understand your hesitation. People have made him out to be bigger than he is. It is by sheer stubbornness my husband has managed to alienate everyone he comes in contact with. Maybe over time you will find something to better occupy your time. Perhaps something where you won't feel guilt."

She thought a moment and remembered a favorite activity from her youth.

"I know! What do you think of my teaching you to sew? What do you think?"

A smile tugged at the young woman's youthful features. "Would you, ma'am? I'd be delighted and I'm a fast learner, don't you worry. Why, all I was ever taught was how to launder, cook, and tend to other people's needs. My grandmother had planned to teach me the ways of sewing, but an epidemic took her earlier than planned. It was probably best; her hands were always shaky."

Evelynn smiled, pleased with her suggestion. "Yes. It's settled. Sewing lessons. I'll have to hunt for some of my old dress patterns, or actually, I'll buy some new ones from the store. With fashion changing all the time it would be grand! We'll get started in a few days. I promise you'll enjoy it, as will I."

She watched Bess slip into the kitchen with an added bounce in her step. Evelynn clasped her hands behind her back and walked around the rooms. When would Brandt learn people liked to feel appreciated, loved, and cared about? His stern face could frighten the snot out of a bull if he looked at it right. He'd be angry with her about wanting to teach Bess to sew, and think her foolish, but she hardly cared. It was her home too.

He should be pleased she wanted to do something to help another person better educate herself and give unselfishly of her time. Early in their marriage, he'd made it clear he preferred her to extend herself to the needy people in town, a role she couldn't see herself do. She didn't treat people as if she was better or above anyone else. It was a role better suited for her husband. Even if he did grumble about her proposition, she was proud of herself for coming up with the idea in the first place and, with or without permission, would find a way to teach Bess in the end. It was the least she could do after all the hard work the woman did. Tolerating Brandt and all his pettiness was work enough.

With a quick glance outside at the fading sunlight, she realized the men would be home soon and immediately went upstairs to check over her appearance. The day had almost gotten away from her and she wasn't at her best. If there was anything more upsetting to her husband it was coming home and seeing his wife look dowdy. He'd often remarked about her state of dress and his expectations of her appearance. She thought it strange considering he rarely looked at her. All her hours of effort were a waste when the intended party ignored them.

A thought swept through her, one that almost made her lose her balance on the stairs. There was one man who looked at her with appreciation behind his eyes. A man whose look peeled away the restrictive layers of her clothing along with layers of her insecurities. A lustful look to bring a slow burn up along her face and blaze deep down into her belly. Her husband only looked through her or beyond her. However he saw her, it left his eyes expressionless and dull. Still, she hoped one day, he would stop and see her for the woman she had grown into. It would mean a great deal and make the difficult years with him seem, for a moment, worthwhile.

Evelynn took her time freshening up, careful to make sure her appearance would be pleasing. She stood before the long oval mirror and smiled approvingly. Her dress had been a gift from a dear friend of hers who had inherited a large sum of money. It was something from Europe and elegant to the touch. The fabric was dyed a pale blue to match her eyes, with puffed sleeves, a neckline and bodice in solid lace, ruffles, and a full skirt with peplum tab at the waistline to camouflage her shapely hips. The hem hung to her new boots, stylishly fastened with side hooks. She was having a difficult time breaking them in and had to wear thicker hose to keep the insides from rubbing against her fragile heels.

A small patch of lace peeked out from beneath the bottom of the dress and made her feel even more like a lady. Brandt never said how much he appreciated the way she looked, but once in awhile he would nod like she were a child pleasing her parents. If this was to be what he considered a compliment, than she received one a few times throughout the year.

Closer into the mirror she looked, mentally erasing the remaining qualities of her youth. Her face was still smooth with tiny wrinkles etched around the corner of her eyes. She was pleased with her long, mahogany hair, framing a peach-toned face with a light spray of freckles along her cheeks and bridge of her nose. Make-up was kept subtle, a request from her husband who didn't understand why women bothered to paint themselves up. She had argued once how contradictory he was. What did he want? To have her look her best or not? It wasn't as though she had many occasions to dress up for. She hoped to make dinnertime more of an event than a routine.

Most of the time she didn't fret about being cooped up in the house, but she had restless moments and found herself on long jaunts around the streets, stopping in the general store to grab something sweet and heading over to the dry goods store to see the latest fashions from Paris when the mood struck. Beyond that, she was a mere fixture in one room or another, with only a minor amount of dust to be looked after.

Comfortable with her appearance, she went downstairs to check on Bess' progress with dinner and to see if she needed any help.

Chapter Four

As her foot hit the final step, the door thrust open and brought in a slight draft of smoky smells. Daniel, her husband's apprentice, greeted her with a polite grin through his heavily smudged face. The poor dear looked as though he'd been worked to death.

"Evening, Mrs. Whitling." Even after a full day his voice was still filled with energy, and it fueled her spirits. Her gaze cast over his long blond hair pulled back into a ponytail and hung to the middle of his back. Loose strands mixed with sweat swept around his face. Dirt coated every stretch of exposed skin along with his thin white top and trousers. She looked up to greet her husband and found his expression set in the usual brooding fashion.

"Tough day, dear?" Evelynn offered a sincere smile but realized it was lost on him.

His gruff voice summed it up as every night. "There's no other day to be had."

"Of course."

"I don't know why you bother to ask the same question each night. My position demands more time than anyone else working in Johnstown."

"Yes, dear."

He started to enter the dining area when she put her arm out, waving her hand frantically.

"Bess cleaned these floors this afternoon. Would you please take off your dirty boots and wear your moccasins?"

He glowered at her. "I'll do no such thing. This is my house and I don't cater to the hired help. It's what the hell I pay her for. Work all day and expect to be given orders..."

His words stung. Not only did he ignore her request, he made it clear how little respect he held for others.

Daniel took a seat on the floor and pulled off his own boots. "I'm happy to dine without my boots. Unless someone objects?"

Evelynn hesitated a moment and looked over at her husband. He was certain to have an opinion on the matter. She decided not to give him the chance. "Don't be silly. Here. You can wear these moccasins. They don't get near enough wear as it is. Besides, it's been usually cool in the evenings as of late and I wouldn't want you to catch your death."

His smile nearly melted the moccasins out of her hands. "Thank you."

He reached up and their hands touched briefly. A slight vibration lingered in her fingertips and traveled up her arm. She directed her glance down at the floor, quickly clasping her hands behind her back. Her body swung as she watched him put on the moccasins. Why did this interaction between them feel comfortable? She could picture herself coming out of the kitchen wearing nothing but an apron around her waist and greeting him at the door with a longing kiss.

"Are we going to stand around all night or do we get to eat? I don't know about anyone else but I've worked up an appetite."

She frowned at her husband's impatience and shook away her torrid thoughts. "Yes, dear."

Evelynn popped her head into the kitchen and gave a reassuring smile at Bess. "The men are home and ready to eat. I apologize for my husband's lack of respect. I will help you with the floors tomorrow."

"Nonsense, ma'am. It is what I am used to doing. Thank you for your thoughtfulness."

With a defeated feeling, she went back into the dining area and watched Brandt take off his coat and hang it on the hook. She waited, half expecting for him to do something completely out of character and acknowledge her, but once again she was disappointed. Not a single smile or admiring word. It confused her how she could hate the man she married more and more each day.

Daniel pulled out a chair and sat down, absently brushing away the strands of his hair from his beautiful face.

She took her place across from her husband and unfolded a napkin, setting it neatly across her lap. Once Brandt sat down, Bess made her rounds, serving stew in the large china bowls along with a platter of stacked high golden biscuits.

"Jam or honey tonight, sir?" The maid's voice quivered as she spoke.

"Jam, unless it's the same kind you served last time. Dreadful stuff. Somewhere between sour and tart."

Evelynn frowned. "I made the jam, thank you. I don't even know why I try."

He looked at her and shrugged. "I don't know what else to say. I didn't like it. You know that cooking isn't your forte. In fact, I don't know what it is you do around here."

She shot an icy glare in his direction and picked up her spoon.

Bess hurried back with honey and hovered a few moments, checking to see if everyone had been properly served. Evelynn nodded approvingly at her and took a bite of stew. As she chewed the tender meat and potatoes, she rehearsed what she would say to Brandt.

When she finished the bite, she leaned forward and cleared her throat, to receive permission to speak. Brandt looked up. A small dab of gravy clung at the side of his moustache. She scraped at her face until he figured out what she meant and wiped it away with his napkin.

"You wanted to say something?" His look was amused, as if she would ever have anything intelligent to add to the table.

"Yes, I did. I wondered if Bess could have time to herself a day or two a week. After she's finished her chores, of course. I should like to teach her to sew."

A childlike pout crossed his face and he set his spoon down. He folded his arms at his chest and leaned back. "Absolutely not. There are too many things to be attended to in this house as it is. Not to mention the garden and laundry. What could she possibly need with extra time? We did not hire her as a companion for you."

Evelynn resisted the urge to fling her bowl of piping hot stew at his face. It was apparent he was skirting around the real issue, his continued annoyance that she didn't take care of the house herself.

Still, she was persistent and wouldn't let him off the hook. "I was thinking for an hour, once or twice a week. It would be advantageous for her to learn how to sew, for herself as well as others. As it is, when you have holes in your garments, you opt to buy new ones rather than have them fixed. This would help save money in the long run, surely you couldn't balk at that." She watched his brow arch and she continued on. "Nothing was said about my need for a companion or Bess avoiding her responsibilities. Honestly, you of all people should know the importance of teaching someone to improve on their skills. It would be the same with what I am doing."

His lengthy stare made her uncomfortable and she nibbled on the corner of a biscuit.

"I'll consider it. Seems a waste of time to me. We house and feed the woman. It's not our duty to promote her hobbies nor to entertain her."

"Forget it." Evelynn stared into her bowl, twisting her spoon around the meat and potatoes in an obscure pattern.

She jumped when he brought his fists down on the tabletop, making the candlesticks quiver.

"Fool-hearted woman! I said I would bloody well consider it. Eat your dinner and quit with the mindless chatter at the table. I'd rather eat my meal than talk nonsense. I work my ass off and come home with a sizeable appetite, only to have you quickly diminish it with your words."

An image of her standing and saluting him came to mind, but she knew better than to draw out his anger. Nothing ruined *her* appetite more than a quarrel where he behaved like a child. It was especially embarrassing when Daniel was at the table watching their normal interaction. She could see it in his eyes he was uncomfortable and she couldn't blame him.

Dinner turned into an endless dance of spoons to mouths. Talk wasn't on the menu once Brandt had declared it. Her feeble attempts at conversation about work were met with aggravated growls and grumbles. From the corner of her eye she watched Daniel and noted his calm repose. His humble, good-natured ways were well received by her, and highly appreciated. She often believed it was Brandt who could use time as an apprentice and learn the fine art of being a gentleman.

When Evelynn had first been introduced to Daniel, he was timid, if not painfully shy, and dreadfully lean. Her husband had teased him about his lack of strength, calling him a twenty-one-year-old girl trapped within a boy's body. Evelynn despised her husband's insensitivity and tried to ease the young man's nerves immediately. There was more to a man than muscles, something she didn't expect her husband to know anything about. Two years later, he had grown into a fine young man. His strength had increased, and it showed in his arms. The lines and angles of his face remained fine and soft, and gave him character. She imagined he would grow old gracefully with a face showing all the wisdom he held. His mystery, youth, and spirit intrigued her.

Bess walked in with a pitcher of milk and walked around the table. "Would anyone care for more?"

Brandt wadded his napkin into a ball and threw it on the table. "I for one am finished. I'll take my whiskey in the parlor." He stood and walked to the sitting room, pausing with his hand on the doorknob. "Daniel, you best be resting. Big day tomorrow."

The young man's head bobbed obediently and he scraped away at the last of his stew. Evelynn abhorred the way he was treated. More like a pet than a person. She feared the abuse he was subjected to would only get worse over the next five years. It was a rough life for an apprentice, being nothing more than a fetch-it boy, under direct tutelage and scrutiny, for seven miserable years.

She knew her husband was an expert blacksmith, but she didn't care for his role as master to anyone, especially herself.

Brandt gave a nod Evelynn's way and disappeared into the small room, closing the door behind him. She despised his parlor with a passion. Not because it was off limits to her, but because of the activities he chose to partake in there. Drinking copious amounts of whiskey and smoking his foul pipe. It reminded her of a bar. The only thing missing were women parading around in their undergarments flashing flesh for cash, or more.

Daniel wiped the corners of his mouth and stood, bowing at her like one would for a princess. "Thank you for the lovely company. The meal was delicious as always."

Evelynn looked away until she was sure the crimson color faded from her face. "You've more than earned it with the way you work, but you will have to thank our dear Bess for the meal. She is amazing in the kitchen."

She wasn't ready for him to leave and tried to think up something...anything to say. "How did your day go?"

"It was tough. I bent a couple rods and got hell for it, of course. Learn as you go, my grandfather used to say. One day I will have my own shop and be the man everyone depends on. Like Brandt. Until then it's the way of things."

"I admire your integrity. It takes a strong person to deal with my husband on a daily basis."

"I can't deny he's hardnosed, but he's a fine teacher. I hope to garner the same respect. I've learned a lot in my time here."

She resisted the yearning to ruffle his hair with her fingers. Such a move would be bold and unladylike. Instead she voiced a question she'd had on her mind.

"You've grown, Daniel. Maturing into a strong man. Have you any lady admirers?"

The question sounded too personal, and yet at the same time she couldn't help but be curious. She held her breath, waiting for an answer she wasn't certain she wanted to hear.

He shrugged and smoothed his hair back, retying it into a ponytail. "I haven't much noticed to be honest. By the time the day is done all I'm thinking about is food and sleep. Don't have much time for women folk."

Her heart cheered selfishly. "Pity. Well, I should be letting you get your rest. Night, Daniel."

He pushed in his chair and walked toward the door.

Evelynn watched him change out of the moccasins and slip his dirty boots back on over his hose. She noticed a tear in his vest.

"Is this recent?"

"It's been torn about a month now. It ripped when I was carrying some farm tools. I'd almost forgotten about it."

She lowered her voice and stepped a little closer. "Leave it with me sometime and I'll be happy to mend it."

He returned with a charming smile. "Thank you for the moccasins, they were nice and warm. Much obliged. Good evening."

Part of her wanted to run to him and embrace his body, bury her head in his smooth, hairless chest and beg to be held. The urge was strong and she worried her eyes did the talking for her. Instead she nodded her head and let the last bit of light in her day fade off as he closed the door. The house was once again lonely and felt more like a cage.

Brandt opened the parlor door and walked into the dining room, the smell of tobacco swirled into the room.

Evelynn sat at the dinner table and waved her hand before her nose. "It's a nasty habit. I wish you'd leave it for outside only."

"Woman, this is my house. Built with my bare hands on land bought and paid for by my blood, sweat, and tears. Don't go telling me where I can and can't smoke. I'm considerate enough to smoke in my parlor as it is. Now quit pestering me with things. I'm tired and need to clean up before I go to bed. Will you be along soon?"

She was excruciatingly tired. Tired of him and the way she lived, but that fight would have to wait for another night. As fatigued as she was, he wasn't the company she wanted. "I have some things to tend to for now. I'll be up later."

"What on earth can't you finish during the day? I have yet to figure out what all you do around here."

She bit her tongue and tried to divert his attention to other things.

"About the sewing lesson with Bess, have you made your decision?"

His glare shifted into an emotionless fog. "Have it your way. If you think it's worthwhile. One hour, once a week. No more. Good night."

She gave him an obedient nod and smiled. At least this fight she'd won. Evelynn watched him make his way to the landing and put his hand on the banister. He groaned over his aches and pains while climbing the stairs. One kiss would have been thoughtful and erase some of the doubt that lingered with her every breath. But no, nothing. Not even a compliment on her dress or how she looked. She was as lonely as before.

With a shake of her head, she hurried into the kitchen to share her good news. Bess was rinsing off the dishes and gasped at Evelynn's swift, unannounced entrance.

"Ma'am, you startled me!"

"You'll forgive me once I tell you my news. I have permission to teach you to sew." She leaned in closer and whispered in her ear. "He said once a week, but what he doesn't know won't hurt him. I'll teach you all I can. We'll start right away. I'll go into town and buy some sewing supplies tomorrow."

Bess threw her arms around Evelynn and immediately pulled back, her lips trembling. "I am sorry, ma'am, it wasn't my place to behave in such a manner."

She waved her hand in the air. "Nonsense. It's not like anyone else hugs me around here. I'm not like my husband. You don't have to walk on eggshells around me."

Inside she soared at the small victory. Little by little she would assert herself. Maybe it was the answer to the strange feelings muddling inside her mind. Perhaps she needed to be more in control and slowly break Brandt down. If she could soften him, there might be a way to save their marriage. Her one remaining question was, was it worth saving?

She opened the back door and looked out at the night sky. Stars littered the never-ending sheet of black, giving her hope for a freedom to be found somewhere. It was a comforting sight. Bess came up behind her, throwing a shawl over her shoulders.

"You'll catch cold out here without this on, ma'am."

"Thank you. Will you ever call me by my first name?"

"No, ma'am. I don't think so."

"I wish you would. I consider you an equal, as well as a friend. I hope someday you will change your mind."

"Yes, ma'am. Dishes are cleaned and put away. I'll do the floors again after the men leave. If you won't be needing me, I'll retire for the evening."

"No, I'm fine. You can't give me what I want."

"Ma'am?"

Evelynn realized she'd spoken out loud and immediately laughed it off.

"Don't mind me. Scattered thoughts. Sleep well. One day you'll awaken in a grand house with a handsome man who loves you and will take good care of you. We were both destined for a better future."

She looked over at the barn Brandt insisted on calling a boarding house. It lay only a few steps away. Her husband had built it as a place for an apprentice to sleep, not wanting the student in his way or enjoying too much of his own residence. It was small with a barn-like interior. There wasn't a real bed but the bundle of hay and blankets was somewhat comfortable, if she imagined it enough. She'd found her own way to make it more comfortable, something Brandt didn't know about, yet. The very structure taunted her. Evelynn hoped Daniel was warm and able to rest. As hard as he worked, she was certain he collapsed into bed and fell right to sleep. The thought of sleep made her eyes heavy and she closed the door.

As she walked up the stairs, the sound of her husband's snoring grew louder. It would be another long night. She undressed in the soft glow of the moon and pulled on her ivory dressing gown. It was hard to imagine if Daniel found her attractive. She'd forgotten what it was like to have a man stare at her and wonder what figure she had. Another glance at the mirror and she felt foolish. What did it matter? She was a married woman. If any man dared look at her, Brandt would surely put them in their place. Evelynn piled her hair on top of her head and crawled beneath the covers. Quietly, she lay down and faced the window. The odor of his pipe clung in the air from his clothes and tickled her nose. Was there anything she liked about the man she shared a bed with each night? Her heart sank as she realized there wasn't.

If there was somewhere she could go on her own, a place to run away to and hide, she would. The house wasn't her home. Somewhere there had to be a place for her, and didn't include Brandt.

"Anywhere but here," she whispered to herself repeatedly until sleep found her.

Chapter Five

Daniel tossed about in his makeshift bed of hay bales and an old, but comfy mattress Evelynn had found for him. The day had been a strenuous one. Brandt insisted Daniel do the bulk of pounding, and now he paid the price. Every muscle in his body ached. He'd hoped to have enough time to clean up properly, but forgot to ask permission to use the tub before his master had retired to his parlor. The only water around came from the well around back and it was cold as ice.

He found it poor manners to eat around the dinner table inside such a beautiful home covered from head to toe in dirt and smelling none too pleasant. Especially when Evelynn Whitling was always such a vision to behold. Always dressed in sensual fitting gowns. They piqued his curiosity to what lay beneath. She was his ray of pure sunshine and unknowingly the one who kept his temper under wraps where his so-called master was concerned.

He didn't know how any apprentice survived the harsh life of being nothing more than a slave in training. Seven years under the direct tutelage and abusive treatment of an unfeeling man hell bent on authority and absolute perfection had the potential to break him.

It was times like these when he wanted to kick himself for having gone against the family trade, but guilt had played its dirty hand. Both his father and grandfather had been master woodcarvers, though it was his grandfather who had the most talent. All of the men in his family were superior craftsmen with their hands, taking a piece of nothing special and turning it into something fit for a king. But after what happened to his sister, he couldn't make it his living. He'd always be reminded of that fateful summer day.

Daniel turned over to his left side and winced. He was certain there was a bruise the size of a melon forming beneath his armpit. Brandt had socked him good for disobeying an order, or at least that was his excuse. All day, every day, it was the same thing. Told to fetch this, fetch that. Pound this, mold that. Crank up the flames, dig more coal, fill the orders, deliver the orders, stand back, hurry up. One backbreaking chore after another. All the while being subjected to the verbal abuse of hearing how stupid, ignorant, weak, and useless he was. It was exhausting. He wasn't one to shy away from hard work, but everything else depleted his spirit. While he was thankful to have learned a lot in a relatively short period of time, it had more to do with the speed in which he picked things up. Even as a young boy he'd been a quick learner.

Whenever he tried to offer his opinion on how to shape a piece of iron differently, he was ridiculed and called stupid. Brandt's temper in general harbored right at the edge, as if he were waiting to have a reason to spill over and take everything out in his way. And it did, more times than he was willing to admit to himself.

While he, as a lowly apprentice, was expected to be respectful and obedient, his own master could behave as ill as he pleased and be praised for it. Most infuriating was not being able to talk about his family. How he missed them. His grandfather had been highly influential for him, a true mentor, teaching him about how a man should conduct himself both in his place of business and in the social scene. But he'd quickly been put in his place for bringing up a conversation about his grandfather. Brandt didn't like idle chatter. Unless it led to an argument.

They bantered incessantly. Daniel recalled how the other day he challenged his master on the way he conducted his business. He pointed out how the blacksmith charged the poor twice what he charged the wealthier families. Brandt had almost sent him flying out the door on his ass. It had been worth it. In fact, he was still proud of himself. He'd almost held his own. His master had not appreciated the comment however.

"I'd say you were taking the food out of the mouths of your most loyal customers," Daniel said.

Brandt had been hammering a tool, but froze in mid-swing. When he turned, Daniel had felt the shivers creep up his back.

"What did you say, boy? I don't believe I heard you correctly."

"Of course you didn't. You never want to hear when you're in the wrong."

He'd ducked and missed being decked along the cheek with an odd-shaped piece of metal.

"It's true. The wealthier men can afford whatever price you give them. You know they wouldn't trust their goods and supplies with anyone else. I have a feeling you use that to your advantage. But the farmers and the less fortunate families, well...you're robbing them."

He watched Brandt's eyebrows clash together in fury and his face turn to a glaring shade of red. "Don't you dare tell me how to run my business! I've been at this far longer than you've learned how to pee standing up. If you don't like the way I do things around here, please leave. I can find someone else who won't be such a bother. I promise not to stop you. By leaving you'll be dishonoring your name and no one will hire you for miles around. Being a quitter suits you."

Daniel remained calm. He knew better than to push further. If he wanted to get anywhere in life, he needed to master his trade. But he'd never treat an apprentice the way he was treated. He'd spent the rest of the day taking out his frustration on horseshoes and broken wagon wheels. Each angry thought echoed along with the clanging of the heavy metal. Still, two days later, his arms were paying the price.

He rubbed his hands together, wondering if he'd ever get them truly clean again. They were stained dark time and time again, especially underneath his fingernails. His hands would never be clean enough to touch Evelynn with, though he wanted to touch her more than anything else. He loved to watch her at dinnertime. She carried herself with ease and grace. Very feminine and proper. There were times she stood tall and proud, and other times she was demure, almost hidden away. He wondered about all the quiet little thoughts on her mind. Brandt never allowed her to speak very much, and Daniel had an idea of how that felt. While dinner was the only time he enjoyed a nice warm meal, her presence did most of the warming. Of his heart.

He especially loved to watch her sip soup in her ladylike fashion and how she tested it to see if it were the right temperature. Her luscious lips set in a perfect O as she blew away the steam. Everything about her was dainty, though he sensed she had a strong defiant spirit inside. He wondered how wild she was when making love.

A series of squeaks broke Daniel's thoughts and he stared hard into the dark until his eyes adjusted. Brill, his small rodent friend, was passing by to see if any crumbs were being offered. He sat up and reached into his pocket for a few stale pieces of bread. Carefully he tossed them to the floor and watched with amusement as it nibbled away. When finished, the mouse sat staring at him, its nose twitching.

"That's all I've got for now, my friend. But tomorrow I will be sure to grab you some more. Sometimes I think you'd be better off fending for yourself rather than relying on me. Of course, I spoiled you early on with those leftovers last week. Two biscuits and a generous piece of pie. I starve myself in order for you to feast."

The mouse squeaked in appreciation and started to clean its face.

Daniel realized sadly how alone he was. All he had was a mouse for company. Without the little rodent, he would have no one to share his innermost secrets with.

"One day I shall tell Bess that if she sees a fat mouse running around, it's all thanks to her good cooking." He laughed and reached down with his palm facing up. Brill scurried right into his hand and sat contentedly.

"You'd really take to the mistress of the house, though I wouldn't be surprised if she screamed when she saw you. Women are funny creatures, aren't they? Why, I know you wouldn't hurt a fly. I can tell you don't like putting yourself in any danger. Which is why you've latched on to me, isn't it?"

The mouse turned its head every which way before staring at him again.

"Evelynn is the one who I'm truly indebted to. Her hospitality has nursed many broken bones and torn muscles. Plus she found me this mattress and convinced her husband I should come in and eat dinner with them. I guess you are indebted to her as well."

He couldn't understand how such a beautiful, caring woman could be with such a monstrous brute of a man. Daniel observed her stand her ground with him on many occasions, but wondered how far her husband would go to get his own way. If Brandt ever raised a hand to her, whether in front of him or not, there would be hell to pay. He staved off the pent up anger and hostility for his master enough as it was, but to see Evelynn in pain would surely get the better of him.

Daniel stretched out his legs. He was restless. There was no getting comfortable tonight, soft mattress or not. Along with his sore muscles, his joints ached miserably. He attributed it to the change in weather. Rain was likely on its way. Perhaps late in the week.

His grandfather had called him a walking barometer, able to tell in his joints and bones when the seasons stopped and started. He yawned and painfully stretched again. His mind wandered from one thing to another, making him dizzy. It would be a long night followed by an even longer day if he didn't get some sleep.

Daniel lowered his hand and watched the mouse scamper to the floor. "Okay little guy, off you go."

He reached for the thick wooden stick he had tucked beneath the bed and found his carving knife. Thoughts of Evelynn played at his mind while he whittled. He imagined the feeling of her body beneath his fingers. Following the shape of her curves to all the secret places she had hidden beneath her many layers of clothing. She was a rare beauty, with a smile that held magical powers. It was a difficult task to take in her womanly form in short, fleeting glances, but he couldn't linger or risk being caught and beaten severely by Brandt. Still, he stole looks whenever he could.

His hands stroked at the texture of the knotted wood. It wasn't right to think about a married woman. In fact, he was completely out of line. He had been raised to know better. But he longed to kiss her. Once. And cherish it for a lifetime. He yawned and pushed the stick back under the bed.

Daniel lay back, using his shirt wrapped up as a pillow to support his sore neck. He turned and looked at the large barn doors, and imagined Evelynn walking through, dressed in a beautiful gown, with ribbons hanging from her hair and flowing behind her—streaks of pinks and blues daring him to pull and uncover the masterpiece beneath.

He pretended she was there now. A look of desperation spread elegantly across her face, her eyes begging for him to not ask questions but answer her with actions. His throat went dry and he couldn't muster up any spit. He coughed, grimacing at the pain. A tug at his pants reminded him how long it had been since being with a woman. Even when he'd been with one, there hadn't been anything emotional to it. They'd simply performed an act among strangers. With Evelynn he knew it would be special. It would be the kind of union between two people where everything else ceased to exist. He blinked his eyes, feeling a layer of sweat build up across his forehead. Though it was nothing more than a dream, it would suffice tonight and get him through the loneliness.

Again he pictured her, this time throwing the doors open, a wild look in her eyes. The desperation had faded and in its place was an animalistic need for her to be with him.

"Take me, Daniel."

"What about Brandt?"

"I don't have to answer to him. What difference does it make anymore? He doesn't love me. I don't think he ever has."

Daniel searched for words of logic. He didn't want her to regret anything they did.

"But do you love him?"

"No. I don't think I ever did. He was a way out. It is obvious now."

"You're a married woman. It isn't right for me to take advantage of you."

She reached behind her back and tugged at the ribbons. Her face screwed up in pain, and in the next instant, she stormed up and turned her back to him.

"Please. Help me with my dress. There's a knot in the ribbons and I can't seem to loosen it."

His fingers briefly brushed against her skin. He pulled back, as if burned by a flame. He'd never felt anything softer.

"I'm afraid to."

She turned to him. Her brows furrowed and she clenched her teeth.

"Daniel. I will have you tonight. Please, don't disappoint me."

Again she turned from him. With her arms crossed, she tapped her toe against the floor, waiting with obvious impatience.

This time his hands raced to work the knot loose, and he watched her gown fall away to expose layer upon layer of silk and satin.

"I'm afraid I'll never find you in all this."

"I can manage this part. How is the mattress?"

"I appreciate the fact you found it."

"I take it you mean it is uncomfortable?"

He shook his head, watching as her petticoats drop to the floor. "No, I was thanking you. It's far better than sleeping on the hay. And far less itchy."

Daniel saw she wanted to smile, but could see she didn't want any idle conversation. She was there for a single purpose. To be made love to. He would give her whatever she wanted. And more.

Evelynn nestled into his outstretched arm. Her warmth clashed against his cold chest. She worked his pants down until they surrounded his ankles. With his feet, he worked them all the way off and underneath the bed.

"Evelynn—I..."

"Shhh. Please, don't try and sway me from what I want."

He smiled. "I wasn't about to."

"Oh." Her eyelashes lowered and he leaned down to kiss her.

"I was going to tell you how beautiful you are. I have seen other women and they lack the immaculate beauty you encompass."

The last garments of clothing removed were her ladies' drawers. His breath caught in his throat.

She pressed her ample breasts against his chest, her nipples hardening against his bare skin.

"Take me, I beg of you. Not like a lady. I am not fragile. Take me swift and don't let up until you are fully exhausted."

He had no intention of giving her anything less than what she wanted. The colored ribbons lay in a pile at her feet. Daniel gathered them up and bound her hands behind her back. A look of approval crossed her wistful features. Her breasts were soft as pillows and he buried his head between them. Her femininity made his cock all the more firm. His lips followed the natural curve of her breast until he reached her nipple. It fascinated him to watch it harden at his touch. He swirled his tongue to draw it further out.

"Don't make me wait," she pleaded, her voice urgent and aggressive.

"Well now, what happened to being a lady?" He turned her around and pushed her to the bed, his hands exploring the roundness of her bottom.

He had wanted this for far too long. "Do you feel my desire for you?"

"Yes," she whispered.

His erection was hard. He rested his cock between the roundness of her bottom and smiled at the tiny gasp she uttered. Daniel stroked her awaiting sex, enchanted with the downy texture of hair framing her entryway.

"Steady yourself as I penetrate through your fragrant heat."

Her legs trembled against his touch.

"We have both waited for a long time."

The realistic visions faded from his memory and he sank into a restless slumber. There his dream was renewed, and had him moaning himself awake several times through the night.

Chapter Six

Rays of golden sunshine cascaded along her otherwise dull bedroom, highlighting the face of the grandfather clock in the corner. Evelynn rubbed the sleepiness from her eyes and sat up, looking around. Eternal frustrations lingered from her sleep, and she wondered when or if she'd ever find the answers she needed.

Brandt wasn't in bed, which didn't bother her in the slightest. Normally she was the first out of bed, but her explicit dreams of Daniel as of late kept her content to stay in her surreal haze for as long as possible. She wondered if she spoke his name in the middle of the night.

Slowly she stretched her arms high above her head. Damn her restlessness. It was almost maddening. She wanted to run around outside in circles and scream through the woods, beating her chest with all her might. She wanted to dive headfirst into a large, deep pond to relieve her anxieties by way of drowning. The severity of the anguished want frightened her. Was she going mad? Cooped up in her home with no one to console her. Her mind was everywhere at once, begging for a freedom she could only imagine. Did other women feel the way she did? Suffer at the hands of time and hope for a change she knew would never come? She feared asking anyone. It was more comforting to believe she was crazy than have someone outright know it.

Afraid she had slept too much of the day away as it was, she got up and looked outside. The day was beautiful with blue skies. A breeze shook the leaves of the poplar trees, giving her a hint it was still somewhat cool. Not summer yet. Big, puffy clouds filled the skies in various shapes and sizes. Off in the distance she could see the first signs of gray. She hoped they were headed in a different direction.

Evelynn took her time getting dressed, putting on her silky drawers, petticoats, corset, a cream-colored dress, bodice, and light jacket. She chose a pair of brown boots and buttoned them up to her mid-calf. Her hair was being uncooperative. She gathered it into a loose bun with a few stray tendrils hanging at the side of her face. Slowly she poured water into the washbasin and ran a damp cloth along her face. The hazy tiredness faded from around her eyes and the fog dissipated from her mind. She rubbed a line layer of tinted salve across her lips to brighten them.

In the mirror she admired her reflection. The clothes weren't her style, but she had no idea what her style was. Her husband expected her to look the part of a well-to-do woman, but she longed to get her hands dirty, take chances, and explore the world around her. He would cringe if she were to dress like a worker.

More and more it was becoming clear she wanted change. Even if it were something small, it would give her a boost of confidence. The sewing lesson was her first step, and she couldn't be more pleased. She made up her mind to get outside and head to town right away. Evelynn grabbed a small satchel and went downstairs.

"Morning, my lovely Bess. I take it Mr. Whitling has left for work."

"Yes, ma'am. Foul mood again today. If you don't mind my saying."

Evelynn laughed. "No, I don't mind at all. He's an insufferable grump twenty-four hours of the day. I do believe he thinks his face will crack if he were to smile."

"Care for toast with your tea this morning, ma'am? I could make a batch of muffins or fry up some eggs. Daniel took off with most of the muffins this morning."

"He did?"

Heat coated Evelynn's face as if she'd been caught thinking explicit thoughts of the young man again.

"Yes, ma'am. He has quite the appetite."

"Oh. Who wouldn't when they are treated to your delicious cooking?"

"Thank you."

There was a long pause and Evelynn realized Bess was awaiting her answer.

"Goodness me, my mind is simply scattered everywhere this morning. I think tea will be plenty. My appetite is still asleep."

"You haven't been eating much, ma'am. I know I shouldn't fuss, you are a grown woman, but you could use a little fattening up. Looking much too thin these days."

"Dear Bess, I appreciate your concern. It's the corset. My hips are enough for two, trust me. I prefer to save my appetite for dinner."

The maid handed her a teacup and saucer and went back to cleaning. Evelynn's hands shook as she walked around the room.

"Mm. The tea tastes especially nice this morning. Very rich flavors."

"Same as every other day. Goodness, are you sure you are okay, ma'am?"

Evelynn looked at her and drew her attention back to her teacup. "What? Oh, my hands. I'm not coming down with anything if that's what you're wondering. No. I'm fine. Do you ever get the feeling you are missing out? Where your insides are at war and you are helpless to find peace?"

"I beg your pardon, ma'am?"

She bit her lip and tried to find a different way to approach her question.

"I don't know if I can explain this right. Do you ever worry you aren't making the right choices each day? That there is a specific path set before you and you are destined to go on it, but every time you take a wrong turn and stray from your path, you are ultimately lost and can never find your way back?"

"I'm afraid your words are much too confusing to me."

Evelynn set her teacup and saucer down and gave Bess a quick hug.

"You're right. I'm not making any sense. Forgive me. I hardly know what I'm saying, myself. I'm terribly restless this morning and think a walk will do me some good. With summer around the corner, it's got me thinking of gardening and buying more flowers. I think I'll go into to town early and see about those sewing supplies. I want to get started with your first lesson right away."

She grabbed a hat from a hook on the wall and pinned it on. Why had she said anything? Now Bess was going to think she was losing her mind. Silly thoughts. They were silly and misguided. She lived in luxury compared to many of the people in town, what right did she have to feel needy?

"I'll be back shortly. While I'm gone, please take out a little time for yourself. Even if it's just to sit down and rock in my chair."

Evelynn opened the door and let the sunrays warm her. She took a big, deep breath, filling her lungs with as much of the freshness she could. As beautiful as it was, she was glad to be wearing a jacket. The breeze had a certain bite to it and lashed at her exposed neck. Now she was sorry she wore her hair up.

The walk to town was peaceful, and much too short for her liking. Along the stoned pathway was an abundance of cherry trees in full bloom. Reddish leaves reflected in the sunlight, the same leaves that would later turn to a handsome bronze once fall was in the air. The fragrant smell from the pink and white blossoms gave her a much needed boost to her step.

Pebbles beneath her feet crunched whenever her heel touched down. Birds sang from their hidden perches and she watched butterflies flit from one flower to another.

Once she reached the center of town, she was surprised to find it bustling with activity at the late morning hour. Large groups of men stood around talking. None of which interested her in the least. Several others shouted loudly, raising their fists up in the air as if out of protest. Figuring it was none of her business, she walked on until she reached the general store. Its bright yellow exterior was always a welcome sight to her eyes.

Inside she found crowds of people standing in front of the display cases. She thought it odd how the usually stocked shelves were close to bare. Even the barrels of flour and sugar were greatly reduced.

"It's good to see you, Mrs. Whitling." She looked up from a basket of apples to find Mr. Jeers smiling at her from behind his thick-rimmed glasses. The smile didn't hide the dark circles beneath his eyes or the pallid color of his skin.

"And a late morning to you as well. Looks busy around here. Something going on I should know about?"

He leaned in close, as if relating a secret to her.

"There's talk about the South Fork Dam again. Seems it isn't meeting regulations. Harris has been appointed to oversee things from here on out, a fact some people aren't too thrilled about."

"I suppose not. He hasn't any experience, has he?"

"Not enough to be in charge. I suppose any of the candidates would have been a poor choice."

"I noticed gray clouds in the distance on my way here."

"A storm is moving east and is expected to drop buckets of water on Nebraska and Kansas tonight. People worry what kind of mess it will bring to us. Everyone's buying up food and supplies out of preparation."

"I see. Well, Johnstown has survived many harsh and unforgiving storms before. I wouldn't worry too much about it. I do hope we would be given plenty of warning if there was trouble."

"Hard to say. There has been a great deal of controversy about the dam these past few months. I try not to think the worst, though. My lovely wife Linda has been ordered to stay in bed by Dr. Tolliver. Her body doesn't seem to want to work the way it used to. I shudder to think what we would do if there was a flood."

Evelynn put her hands over his and gave him a soothing pat. "Don't you worry your sweet head about it. This place can make it through anything Mother Nature wants to throw at us. I have faith in the ways of nature, everything happens for a reason."

"You're a sweet woman, Mrs. Whitling. I am sure Linda would want me to say hello from her."

"Please give her my greetings and blessings as well. I'm off to check the post and visit the seamstress. I've decided to start sewing again and would like to buy up some new patterns. Have a wonderful day, Mr. Jeers."

She stepped out of the way of a hoard of customers coming in and quickly made her way to the post office. It didn't make any sense to her, fussing over a storm. The dam was sturdy, she was certain of it. She realized it had been ages since she'd last gone to a town meeting. Brandt always said she should pay attention to what goes on around her, but meetings in the past bored her to tears. People argued, everyone talked at once, and no solution was ever found. And it all came down to a lack of support and money. Those who had money were unwilling to part with it. Poorer folks couldn't do much and were frowned upon. Even Brandt refused to part with his money.

Evelynn patiently waited her turn behind a small line of people sending out mail to their loved ones. Talk of the dam was on the lips of everyone. When it was her turn, she put on her most courteous of smiles.

"Morning, Norma. Don't suppose you have any mail for me? I've been meaning to get over here since last week but I've been busy."

"Looks like your catalogues from Paris came in. There are always such beautiful things inside. Elegant and dainty."

"Yes, indeed they are. But horribly overpriced. I could never afford such extravagant things; even the fabric to make them with is far too much. But it's nice to look and dream. How have you been?"

"Oh. Same as usual. My Henry has been working his poor fingers to the bone at the sawmill. There are frequent accidents around there, which has him doing the work of five men right now."

Evelynn looked around uneasily. She'd always been uncomfortable around Norma. Their family was always struggling to get by with five children to tend to, each one a year apart. They lived in a rickety house on poorly producing property for two years straight, and worst of all she was married to a man who was blind in one eye. Evelynn found herself unsure how to behave or respond.

"I'm sure things will work out. Give Henry my best."

Norma's smile faded slightly. "Yes, I suppose they will. Goodbye, dear."

Evelynn turned and walked away quickly, less impressed by the fancy catalogs now. While they weren't rich, Brandt made much more money than anyone else around. She didn't like it when people thought her a snob, or rubbed her husband's wealth in her face. Not always with words, but also by actions.

With her head held high, she rushed off to see Judy about the sewing items she would need. Grace Magda and Dorothy Brownridge were walking up the pathway toward her. They looked to be in the middle of an animated conversation, and she knew it was all gossip. She decided to pretend to be busy enjoying the scenery and not pay them any attention. Evelynn successfully managed to pass by them and she grinned as they called out to her.

Their kind of talk was nothing but lies and rumors, and she didn't like being made privy to them.

Before they had a chance to catch up to her, she ducked into the seamstress shop and fingered through several spools of thread. She chose some dark colors and turned her attention to a basket of dress patterns. Some where outdated in her opinion, but a couple caught her eye. Her old friend Judy had been busy helping a pair of elderly ladies, and finished up with them.

"Why Evelynn Whitling! I never thought I'd see you in my shop. Where have you been hiding yourself?"

She thought the world of Judy, except for the way she spoke in a loud, shrill tone. They had struck up a friendship many years before, but had both went their separate ways soon after marriage.

"Now, now. I popped in not even six weeks ago. You weren't here. I'm afraid I don't have any good excuse why I haven't been in since."

"What brings you in today?"

"I've decided to take up sewing again."

"Wonderful. I imagine your husband needs his garments stitched all the time."

"He's been buying new clothing because I haven't had the supplies and it's costing us a fortune. I decided to remedy the situation."

"Good thinking. What kind of patterns are you looking for?"

"A feminine gown. Certainly not as extravagant as what I'm wearing."

Judy fingered Evelynn's dress with envy.

"From Europe, isn't it? They have such a way over there."

"Yes. I have a friend who sends me her hand-me-downs. I have to admit, it isn't my style. Much too formal and not always the easiest to get around in. I don't care for the restrictive corset but without it the dress hangs on me funny."

"What fabric are you looking to use?"

"The poly/cotton blend or moiré fabric if you have any on hand. I'll also need some lace for the white cuffs and falling collar."

"Excellent. We have plenty in the store."

"Oh, and some ornamental piping on the seams might be a bit much, but I like the way it looks all the same."

She'd forgotten how much she liked to sew and couldn't wait to get started. In fact, she'd forgotten many of the things she once used to do. What had become of all her dreams?

"Will you be requiring anything else?"

"No, not at this time. Maybe after I do some sewing I'll take up looming. I saw a beautiful loom in the weaver's shop several weeks ago. Beautiful thing. As I watched Annie weave, I saw how calm and relaxed she was. Peaceful. I was jealous."

"Do you think Brandt will object?"

Evelynn shrugged. "I don't know why it would concern him. We are from two different worlds, he and I."

Judy gave her a strange look. "Are you and Brandt having problems?"

Once again she'd found herself talking out loud to others. "I'm sorry. You mustn't mind me. We are doing fine. What I had meant was, he works very hard, which leaves me with plenty of time to keep myself busy. I think sewing will be my new passion."

She was relieved Judy didn't press her for more. Instead her friend brought out all the items she'd asked for and started tallying them up.

"Comes to fifteen dollars even. If you need any more patterns, let me know. I will take some of my favorites and put them in a separate drawer. It will keep all your patterns unique."

Evelynn rummaged around her satchel until she found the right amount of change.

"Sounds great. Thank you, Judy. It was lovely to talk with you."

"Same here. Don't be such a stranger."

"I won't."

She tucked the bundle of fabric and lace beneath her arm and started on her way home. James, the tanner, nodded as she passed by and again she glanced into the weavers to watch Annie busily looming away with the same blissful look on her face she wore last time. Evelynn imagined she, herself, wore the same blissful look when she thought about Daniel. A rush of blood raced through her body and made her catch her breath. The thought of him indeed took her breath away.

At the last minute, she took a side road and decided to pay a visit to the two hardworking men. It would give her a good excuse to see Daniel in action. As she approached, the smell of melting steel and iron held fast in the air.

Chapter Seven

She used to come watch the young apprentice work all the time, hiding away in the shade to keep from being seen. Daniel was dressed in brown leather pants with buttons on the shins, hose, and a white long sleeve shirt rolled up to his elbows. He looked handsome in his red vest and leather apron. Around his neck he wore a handkerchief in deep red. He said it was given to him by his sister as good luck. She liked to watch him from afar as he cast, bent, welded, and riveted fireplace racks, pothooks, locks, utensils, and decorative wrought iron. His muscles rippled as he pounded on the anvil.

The shop was enormous with poles protruding from the walls with rows of giant tongs, chisels, hammers, and various other tools hanging from them. Inside the forge was a raised brick hearth with bellows around it to feed the soft-coal fire and a large hood to keep away the smoke.

Evelynn watched him work the charcoal, bringing the flames high to melt the steel. There wasn't much concern in getting caught in the act; the shop was always dark.

When she was first married, she used to come and watch people bring in broken household items to be fixed, horseshoes, agricultural implements, and hardware. Once or twice someone brought in wagon wheels and carts. The village wouldn't have made it without Brandt, and she learned early on how he liked holding such power. She was also smart enough to know it worked both ways.

Evelynn peered inside the shop and watched Daniel heat, temper, strike, sharpen, and cut the metal. Expertly he handled each piece with delicate care. She loved the way he laid his tongue in the corner of his mouth while he hammered the tools.

Before she had a chance to speak, she heard Brandt shout, and it made her breath catch in her throat.

"You are nothing but a useless idiot! I should stick your head in the fireplace to help get some sense into you, boy. You'll be working off the price of everything you've ruined. I can't figure out why in the hell you bother trying! Careless, careless boy. Too many of my pieces have been broken or misplaced since you became my apprentice. And you want to be a blacksmith one day? You'll never get anywhere. You'll be the laughingstock of the whole village. Mark my words, you won't have the chance to run your own shop."

"I'm sorry, sir."

"And where the devil is my prized anvil?"

"Which one do you mean?"

"My favorite one. Don't be stupid."

She watched Daniel hunt all over the shop trying to find it.

"I don't see it."

"As far as I'm concerned, you took it."

"No. I didn't. I wouldn't take your tools, I swear."

"It's never gone missing before."

"Not true. I've watched you misplace it plenty of times."

"But I've always found it. I was using it yesterday. Are you trying to get back at me?"

Evelynn couldn't believe her husband was accusing Daniel of stealing! She bit her lip, hoping the tool would be found and the argument would end soon.

"What would I get back at you about?"

"For not letting you have your way. For not letting you spout your grandfather's stories. Who knows! Ungrateful is what you are."

"I am most grateful for everything you teach me."

"What thanks do I get? I am sure you are aware that I have the nicest house here. And it's very considerate of me to allow you a room in the boarding house."

"It's the nicest barn I've ever seen."

"It's a boarding house."

"I've never complained and I'm not complaining now."

Their voices started to get louder. She watched as several passersby glanced over and walked swiftly away from hearing range.

"You remember, young man, it is by my wife's good graces I let you eat with us inside the house at all. If I had my way, you'd be eating scraps."

"Yes, sir. You like to remind me often."

"Don't give me lip. I still believe you stole my anvil. I'll expect you to take your punishment like a man and I'll be docking your pay considerable over the next month to pay for it."

Evelynn had enough. She stormed inside the shop and strode right up to Brandt.

"What is all this? Did you know everyone from miles around is able to hear you belittle your apprentice?"

"What business is it of yours?"

"Daniel works himself to the bone for you and all you can do is criticize his every move? As if you don't have plenty of tools of your own. You are a master with these tools; you can make yourself new ones. Docking his pay or feeding him table scraps? I won't stand for it!"

The fire in her husband's eye rivaled the fire blazing nearby from the hearth. He took hold of her arm and pulled her outside. The sudden descent from the dark to light temporarily blinded her. Still, she stood her ground.

"Woman, this is not your place. Do I tell you how the house should be run?"

"Yes, as a matter of fact you do. I still can't figure out why you consider yourself all high and mighty. The way you look down on other people, it's disgusting."

"I will not listen to your nonsense. Without me, people wouldn't be able to tend to their crops. I keep the farming business where it's at."

"No, my dear husband. You forget. Without the people, you would have no purpose. They come to you with their items to be mended, certainly, and their weapons to be fixed, but you in turn need them as well."

He grunted and gripped her tighter, making her drop the bundle of fabric and her dress pattern. "No wife of mine will come in here and make a fool of me. You understand? Your place is in the home, which is where you should be right now!"

"I had errands to run and came by to say hello. Don't go spouting off your vulgarities to me because you are sore at Daniel. I will not be spoken to this way in public."

She glowered at him and picked up her purchases. Without another look his way, she turned and started walking home. With her head down, she had almost made the mistake of running over Grace and Dorothy, who she had no doubt witnessed the whole thing.

They stood silent in the street, their mouths agape. Looking around, Evelynn noticed several other people, all wearing puzzled expressions on their faces. People were certain to spread rumors how her marriage was in trouble or the way she stood up for Daniel. Either way, the gossip would be true for once. She and Brandt were having problems and she was infatuated with Daniel. Evelynn lifted up her skirts and stormed home, muttering words about her husband's insensitivity.

෨ ෨ ෨

Hours later, she'd calmed down and had Bess bring her some tea with honey. She stirred the spoon around, watching the creamy color swirl. What kind of man did she marry? It was one thing to mince words with *her*, they had little in common, but to berate Daniel in front of others for them to hear? It was unprofessional at best, and she'd make sure her voice was heard on the matter. The problem was at some point her bravery left and she rarely had the last word. For Brandt it was about who could shout the loudest and whose voice made the very walls tremble. Sometimes he would threaten to throw her out with nothing. She often wondered how far he would go. He was a man who concerned himself with what others thought, so she decided he wouldn't. Unless she pushed him to his limits.

Bess walked by a third time, wringing her hands tightly.

"Come sit down a minute with me. Why are you nervous?"

"I don't mean to disturb you, ma'am. I was concerned about you."

Evelynn put a hand to her chest, her eyes wide. "Whatever for?"

"The look on your face and your muttering when you walked in. Did something bad happen?"

"Oh goodness no, not anything new anyways." She laughed and did her best to resume a softer expression. "Once again Brandt and I mixed words. I tire of his laws and rules he feels govern my life as if I haven't a mind of my own. By my own good nature I stopped by to say hello and all I received was grief and a verbal lashing. It was embarrassing to say the least, others could hear it."

"I am sorry, ma'am."

"Nothing to be sorry over. I suppose I could be one of those docile wives who keep their mouths shut, all thoughts to themselves, nod, and live completely through their husband. I wasn't raised in such a fashion and I'm not ever going to change. He's never respected my opinions and I have more brains in my head than he does. All he has is muscle."

Bess stifled a giggle and Evelynn broke out into laughter.

"Oh my, listen to me go off. The sad thing is, I haven't even gotten started. If Brandt knew all the things I wanted to say to him, I'd be banished from this house for good. Enough about that. I went to see Judy today and picked out a pattern I think you'll like. I also got some nice fabric, but I will need to dust it off first. I had hoped to get started today but my head is still pounding from earlier."

"No worries, Mrs. Whitling. I appreciate you wanting to take the time to teach me."

"I most certainly do. It's resurrected my love for it. In fact, once I've taught you to sew, I am going to buy a loom and show you how to work it too. My momma taught me but it's been ages. I'll have to re-teach myself, I think."

She finished her tea and set the cup and saucer in the kitchen. "It smells divine in here. What do you have planned for dinner tonight?"

"Roast chicken with rosemary, potatoes with parsnip, glazed carrots, and a field green salad. Peach pie will be for dessert if anyone has room."

"My mouth is watering now! I'll look forward to it. Prepare for it to be quiet at the dinner table. My husband will be most displeased."

Chapter Eight

Daniel finished cleaning up the tools, still searching for the missing anvil. He didn't know if it was missing, if Brandt himself was testing him to see if he was honest, or if someone had actually come in and taken off with the damn thing. He'd picked up some leather pouches from the tanner earlier. There had been plenty of time for Brandt to hide something. One thing was for sure, Daniel was in for a beating and it wasn't going to be painless.

The image of Evelynn coming to his rescue helped put a smile on his face. She was all dress and petticoats, bursting in like a beautiful storm. He was used to fighting his own battles, but it was amusing to see her try to dissuade her husband. She had some fire to her, or at least when she wanted to.

Brandt covered up some of the tools and turned around, practically towering over him.

"I'm giving you another chance to come clean. Did you steal my anvil or not?"

"No."

"Liar. Maybe you'll remember where you've hidden it while we are eating supper around the table and you are not."

Daniel gritted his teeth. "If you think it's best."

"I do. Now let's head home."

As they walked through the town in the early evening light, Daniel was careful to keep a few steps behind Brandt. The blacksmith had a problem with him walking too closely. He watched the way he'd smile and nod at the people he passed. It made Daniel sick to see him acting like a pompous ass.

When they walked up the path to the blue, two-story house with white trim, he made a quick beeline to the barn. Unfortunately Brandt was right behind him.

"Hold up. We have unfinished business. I'm going to have to teach you a lesson about lying and thievery. In my shop, there will be neither."

Daniel smirked. He couldn't believe what he was hearing. His own master lied and stole from people every single day. Prepared to show he was unafraid, he walked in first and lit the lantern, turning the flame up high enough to where they could see. Brandt struck him hard against the cheek and pushed him in the middle of his ribcage. A bale of hay broke his fall and allowed him to get up easier.

"A man shouldn't lie to another man. It's dishonorable. I demand respect and however I have to enforce it, I will! As a reasonable man, I offer you one final chance to come clean. I won't punish you if you tell me the truth. What do you have to say for yourself?"

"I didn't take it. I would never do such a thing. I suspect you hid it while I was out running errands."

Brandt raised his fist. "I don't have time for lies, boy. I work and I work hard."

"I don't know what to tell you. I didn't touch it."

"I have no other choice."

Daniel tired of the abuse. He could see it in his master's eyes, he was out for blood, and wouldn't be satisfied until a drop of Daniel's was shed.

"I understand. You do what you need to do. I'm a strong lad and can take anything you dish out to me."

A wicked smile danced across the blacksmith's face. "Then so be it."

He took off his belt and slapped the leather against the palm of his hand. A loud snap echoed.

"Turn around and take it like a man."

Daniel turned and rolled up his shirt exposing his back and shoulders. He stared straight ahead at the far wall, watching Brandt's shadow as he raised his belt.

The first strike hardly made him flinch. Leather against flesh. He resisted the urge to make a sound, reminding himself that his strength of character couldn't be easily dismissed. The second one hissed through the air like a snake and left a small bite. Daniel refused to back down, holding his breath and tensing up his muscles. Nothing the man did would make him break. He imagined the look on Brandt's face, as the punishment session wasn't going the way he wanted.

"You're a tough one, are ya? Well, we'll see how much more you can handle after this next one. I planned to start easy on you, but now I'm all warmed up..."

It took the fourth strike with the belt to bring the beginnings of a tear to his eye. It was a tear for Evelynn and how much he'd miss seeing her at dinnertime. There'd be no sunshine in his day now.

"I know you felt that one. This next one here is going to pack some heat."

When the end of the belt made contact against his now welted flesh, he had no choice but to cry out. It wasn't due to weakness, but the pain was beyond the threshold he was ready to withstand. The stinging sensation would be his company for the remainder of the night. His jaws clenched and unclenched as he fought to control his anger. He knew he was fast enough to turn around and take possession of the belt. But he knew it would only be disastrous later on. Instead he said the words he knew his master wanted to hear.

"Enough. Please, I beg you."

"You are lucky. I am feeling generous and damn starved. There will be only five lashings today. I suggest you think about what you have done. I expect an apology come morning."

"Yes. I will think things over."

"Remember. A real man takes his punishment. He doesn't quit. You need to grow yourself a tougher skin if you ever plan to have your own place someday. I can help you. A blacksmith is the king of the town and the most revered. Even if inside they hate you, they will still love you. Without you, they have nothing. They would all be poor. They need you like air."

Brandt put his belt back on and tucked in his shirttails.

"Don't you go telling Evelynn about this. Or I'll decorate your front the same way. Get some rest. You're going to need it."

Daniel could see the gleam in his eye. The man wasn't sorry. He liked reminding him who was boss.

"I'll bring you some fruit in the morning. Maybe a biscuit if Bess makes any extras. You'll need your strength. Tomorrow I'm going to work you extra hard for the added discomfort you brought to my reputation today."

"Yes, sir."

Daniel's stomach lurched at the mere mention of food. Poor Brill would go hungry tonight too. It would be another long, restless sleep for him.

"Good night."

"Good night, sir."

When he was alone, he pulled off his shirt to keep from getting blood on it. He shuddered to think what shape his back was in. The welts would stick around for a long time. He hoped the wounds wouldn't get infected. He sucked in his breath, trying to think beyond the pain. Anger was all he could summon.

"Bastard!"

Daniel kicked a metal bucket and sent it flying to the other side. He gritted his teeth while pummeling a barrel of seed with his fists until a large gash appeared and half of it poured out into the hay.

"I have to get away from here!"

It wasn't the life he wanted to live. It wasn't too late to master another trade. Or was it? Apprentices started young. He'd been lucky to find someone at all given his age. What he thought was the path to good fortune had turned into a path of an inner meltdown waiting to happen. He didn't figure his father would be very proud of him right now. But his grandfather would. He'd tell Daniel he was right in being honest and still accepting the beating. To hold his tongue and let the truth present itself. There was another side to the truth. He couldn't leave. Not yet anyway. If he did, it would be like giving in to Brandt and his abusive ways. It would be quitting in the eyes of his master. He knew the truth, and in time the proof of who took the anvil would come to fruition.

Daniel sat on the bale of hay and chipped away at the thick wood with his pocketknife. Violence wasn't his way, but the thoughts going through his mind were far from tame. All it would take would be a single slit along Brandt's throat and the nightmare would be over. No, he couldn't think such things. His grandfather would turn in his grave if he could hear his thoughts.

He carved carefully along the sloping handle of the stick. It was coming along nicely, taking shape of a cane. Old memories came back to haunt him. All she'd wanted was to walk again. Why had he let her fall?

Chapter Nine

When the door of the house opened, a wind of ferocity filtered into the house. Evelynn braced herself for another round of her husband's angst. He stomped in and flung his soot-covered body into the chair, again forgetting to remove his mud encrusted boots, a permanent scowl imprinted on his face. She waited for the door to open again, but it remained shut. Panic set in.

"Where's Daniel? Was he hurt at work? Will he be along soon?"

"No. He won't be dining with us tonight."

"Is he hurt?"

"He won't be eating with us. Enough said."

"It is not. I want to know why."

Brandt rubbed his forehead. "If you must know, I denied him supper."

"You can't starve him!"

"I can do whatever I want around here. He is still being punished from today. I want to know what you were thinking coming into my workspace and opening fire on me. You humiliated me."

"You? Think about poor Daniel. I think he takes more abuse from you than is right."

"I don't make him stay."

"Of course not. You can't get anyone to stay. This is your third apprentice and the other two barely made it passed one year. Is this the kind of record you'd like as a professional tradesman?"

"It's not your business to concern yourself with."

"It is when I have to deal with you and your temper. It affects me when you outwardly treat another individual under your tutelage with such disrespect that you'd yell at him in front of other people. And it most certainly affects me when you shout at me in public. You only know how to push people away."

"You don't know what you're talking about."

"No, I suppose not. Seven years with you would drive any soul to run away."

He scooted his chair forward and slammed his arms along the table. "You don't say?"

Evelynn nodded her head. "Yes, I do."

"If you think you can do better, then I expect you to pack up in the next few months as we move on to our seventh year together."

"Don't tempt me."

The words were out before she had a chance to leash them up and pull them back.

"From this point on you are forbidden in my shop. Period. Do you understand?"

"Fine. After your horrid display earlier, I expect no one will go there."

"Like all the other gossip in town, the talk will slowly start to fade away and life will resume its normalcy."

"You don't care, do you?"

"Are we discussing our marriage, my shop, or my apprentice?"

"Take your pick. They are all up for discussion."

"I'm not sure why you're concerned with Daniel's welfare. It's not like he does anything around here. He doesn't put food on our table, he costs us money."

"I'm a person who cares about others in general and I don't care to see anyone be mistreated. He wants to learn from you. He wants to become a blacksmith someday and provide for his own family. Let's hope he doesn't pick up any of your unpleasant traits in the process."

She sensed if steam could shoot out of his ears, it would.

"Let's get something straight. Daniel won't make it with me the full seven years. No apprentice will. I'm the best in the business and I aim to stay as such. I'll not have someone outdo me."

The shock from his words nearly barreled her over. She pulled out the chair and swiftly sat down.

"I don't understand. Are you nothing more than a heartless monster? He wouldn't be able to start his own business up anywhere near you. I'm not stupid."

"I'm protecting my assets. The less blacksmiths around, the more business comes to me."

"You're being a selfish pig is what you're being!"

Brandt stood and turned to face the kitchen.

"Bess, Bess!"

"Yes, Mr. Whitling."

"Serve me my dinner in the parlor. I've had enough with the present company for tonight."

"Yes, Mr. Whitling. Right away."

Evelynn grabbed a plate and tossed it to the wall. "You are nothing but a coward," she hissed.

Brandt stormed over and brought his face up close to hers. "We are through with this discussion tonight. I will not come home and be treated with such rude conduct. Mind your manners and bite your tongue woman, or you will find yourself penniless and alone sooner than you would like."

He kicked one of the chairs clear to the other side of the room and went into his parlor. The loud slam of the door vibrated in her ears for several minutes. Her whole body shook as it continued to process the new information. He wasn't just a selfish pig; he was a monster!

Bess hurried with a large plate of food. She stood outside the door and knocked, waiting for him to open it.

"Sir, I have your dinner."

He opened it long enough for her to set things down on the small table by his reclining chair, and he closed it back up, slamming it harder than before.

Bess' eyes were big as saucers. Evelynn could tell she was frightened and unsure of which member of the household to show her loyalty to.

"Ma'am, did you want me to serve you now?"

"I'm afraid I've lost my appetite. Seems to be a regular event around here."

"I'm sorry, would you like a cup of tea?"

Evelynn grabbed the maid's hand and led her into the kitchen. A plate piled high with food sat ready to be served.

"It all smells wonderful. I'd like to take some food out to Daniel. I'm not about to let him starve after a full day's work. He needs his strength. If my husband should ask of my whereabouts, which I'm certain he won't for several hours, let him know I am resting. Please?"

"Yes, ma'am."

"Under no circumstances can you tell him where I am."

"I understand. Be careful."

"I intend to."

Chapter Ten

Brandt stabbed at his food with the fork, piercing it like he was spearing a fish. Damn woman! Wasn't it enough he provided for her, built her a glorious house to do with as she pleased, and made sure she was tended to? He hired a maid and let her have her way with the sewing lessons. What more did she need? She was selfish and ungrateful. The only problems in their marriage were the ridiculous fantasies she had about it.

When he'd been growing up, there hadn't been love between his mother and father. One worked the fields while the other worked the house. They were a unit and relied on one another to get things done. Winters were harsh and crops needed to be tended to. There wasn't time for silly notions of romance. If the work didn't get done, there was no food on the table. His youth had been all about lessons and he wasn't going to make the same mistakes. He had made something of himself. He wouldn't go hungry or rely on the weather for a good crop that year or not. She was blind to the things he showed her every day. He had spoiled her with things early on and now she expected more. Damn her expectations!

What about what he wanted out of the marriage? A wife to come home to who was happy to see him. A wife who was proud of him and all his accomplishments. To come at him with her arms wide and take his coat and help pull off his boots. Was it too much to ask? Instead she stood back and greeted him from afar and let him know about every little thing she disliked about him.

They shared a bed, nothing more. The last time he'd tried to touch her, she'd recoiled and said she wanted to sleep. In the times before, she had sounded unsatisfied and he'd stopped trying. He wasn't cut out to be a husband. He knew it. His whole life centered on his being a blacksmith. It was his identity. The job was tough and thankless and didn't allow for interactions with a woman. His father had pressed upon him the validity marriage gave to his position, especially among the community. He'd fought it, but in the end he made the decision.

Evelynn had been the most beautiful woman in the town. She came from a large family and he trusted she would be equipped with the knowledge to cook, clean, and attend to a home. Young, unblemished, and a figure fit for birthing children. She had the qualities he figured would make her a good wife. In the beginning, she knew her place and did her best to please him. But something happened along the way and he wasn't certain what it was. Day in and day out he'd replayed it in his mind. What had changed her? And why? If she wanted to leave him, it would have to be her doing the leaving. He would not give her the satisfaction any other way.

The food sat in front of him hardly touched. He'd been famished but now his stomach was tied up in knots. It had been a long time since he'd sat down and actually enjoyed a meal. The tension at the table was always high. He could hardly chew his food, let alone swallow and let it digest. At least he had his parlor to escape to.

Brandt lit his pipe and pulled the smoke in hard through his teeth. It burned at his throat in a pleasing way. The smoke curled up and twirled above his head. Yes, he liked his parlor. It was his place to find a moment's peace in his own home. Away from the clatter of Bess' dishes and the scrutiny of his wife. But sadly, he realized what else it kept him from. Apologies.

All their unfinished arguments pinged at his door, trying to get in, but he kept them away until they disappeared into the floor, waiting for the day he would acknowledge their existence. By avoiding the fights he didn't have to apologize, or keep up the banter until he would cave. She wasn't a stupid woman, but she didn't behave the way he wanted.

Brandt put his feet up on the table and rested his head against the back of the chair. Changes needed to be made, but he wasn't ready to face them. He didn't have the time or energy. His mind didn't work the way hers did. Whether she wanted to or not, Evelynn would have to wait. Things would continue as they were. Routine worked well for him. It was all he had. A daily routine. Get up, go to work, eat dinner, smoke his pipe, and go to bed. Maybe one day he could find a way to include her in his routine, but for now she was only in his way.

His anger disappearing along with the smoke from his pipe and he got up to open the door.

"Bess?"

The portly woman waddled out from the kitchen, the sleeves of her dress soaked with water and her face flushed.

"Yes, Mr. Whitling?"

"I'll have my pie now."

"Yes, sir. I will be right in with it."

He put out the pipe and sat back down, the door open a crack to hear her coming. It concerned him how much his wife cared about Daniel's well being. He didn't know if he should be concerned of her nurturing of him, or if it was a common mothering factor. He'd given up all hopes of having a son to continue on his name and business, he wasn't about to press Evelynn about it. She'd made it clear they were distant with one another and he couldn't force himself on her. The truth was, he cared for her, but to what extent was a difficult question. To say he loved her didn't sit right. He tolerated her, looked after her, and was attracted to her. But he wasn't built to love. She was a part of his life, a fixture in the house, but she was hotheaded and provoked him all the time.

Still, there was something about the way Daniel looked at her during dinner. He knew better than to ignore his instincts and they'd been making themselves heard. Brandt had wanted to teach the young man a lesson and he'd let his temper get the best of him. Once he'd gotten started with the belt, he found it hard to stop.

The sound of the leather against the young man's skin was delicious. Each red mark and welt brought him a huge sense of satisfaction. His father had punished him in the same way, and it taught him lessons early on. Daniel needed toughening up, he was far too soft.

A knock at the door interrupted his thoughts and he pushed the door open to let Bess in.

"Here's your pie, Mr. Whitling. I'll take your other plate if you're all done."

"I am. Where's Evelynn?"

"I believe she said she was resting."

"I see."

"If you have everything, I will leave you to your parlor."

He closed the door and sat back down. Maybe he'd try and talk to her a little later when he'd straightened out his thoughts more. Brandt took a large bite of the pie and let the delicious fruit melt in his mouth. If only he'd married someone more like his hired help and not been blinded by Evelynn's charm and beauty. Her blue eyes had mesmerized him and made him forget who he was. She would need to learn her place, like Daniel. A forceful hand was sometimes the only way to go. He would get his way.

Chapter Eleven

With a little bit of everything scrunched together on a small plate, Evelynn went to the makeshift boarding house and knocked lightly. Daniel opened the door, his hair disheveled and only wearing his trousers. A troubled look passed quickly as he broke into a smile. She quickly grabbed the plate with her other hand to keep from dropping it.

"Mrs. Whitling, I beg your pardon. One moment and I will make myself more decent."

She knew she should have turned around to give him privacy, but her curiosity had won out. Instead she watched him put on his shirt, slow and deliberate. Her eyes memorized every line and curve of his sturdy physique. His muscles were toned, strong bulges aglow by the light of the lantern.

"I did not know you would make your presence here. I apologize for answering as I did. It was not my intention to offend you."

She arched her eyebrow. Offend? That had hardly been the case. Aroused, most certainly.

"It is I who must apologize for not announcing my arrival to you. In any case, no harm was done. I wanted to bring you some of tonight's dinner. Please accept it. Bess has made a mouthwatering meal and it has hardly been touched."

Evelynn noticed the way his eyes lingered on the food.

"But...I was given explicit instruction to not eat tonight's supper. I am being punished."

"He said you couldn't eat dinner with us at the table. I decided to bring dinner to you."

She set the plate on a block of wood and sat on an old carriage seat.

"Daniel, there's some things you may have overlooked in your time with us here. I don't share my husband's desire to whip someone into shape, punish or humiliate them, or use power, social standings, or physical strength over others. Brandt has some warped idea of how things should be, but they don't have anything to do with me. I won't have him deciding who does and doesn't eat. Granted I couldn't sway him to have you eat inside with us, but I will see to it you are present at the dinner table tomorrow night."

"You don't have to..."

"Let me finish, please. Whatever squabbles go on at work, I can't do much about them, but here in this house, I do have a say. I am nothing more than an image for him. It is not as though we have any real emotions for one another, though I've tried to love him. Blacksmiths aren't single men, they are married, or they lose value in the eyes of the citizens. People like to believe he is a well-to-do man, with morals and ethics. To him that translates to being married, with the house and servants to do his bidding."

"I did not realize all of this."

"Of course not. I have learned over time to play the games and put up the front to others to keep the peace. At the same time, it's been wearing on me and I'm unable to keep up appearances anymore."

She wanted to tell him about what Brandt said, and how he wouldn't become an apprentice through him, but she couldn't bring herself to say anything. Yet. He looked like something had been troubling him when he answered the door and she didn't want to make things worse. It was strange how easy it had been to open up with him and spill all the emotions she'd carefully been stuffing away inside her. Had her sudden loss of appetite been due to stuffing herself full of anger every night?

Daniel picked up the plate from the wooden block and took a large bite of the fluffy white potatoes.

"Bess is a fabulous cook. Please tell her I have never eaten better since I've been here."

Evelynn smiled. He was always courteous and would make a fine husband someday. If only she had found a man as genuine in the beginning. Things would be different now.

"I shall. She is such a delight to spend time with. I consider her more of a friend and not a maid."

She realized she was rambling and decided it was time to leave.

"I best let you be to eat your supper. Please...don't tell Brandt I was here. He wouldn't understand. If you hide the plate somewhere...say in the corner, I will come fetch it after you two have left."

"I won't say anything."

"Good. It's better if you don't. With his temper and all."

She got up and headed toward the door. "I am sorry for the humiliation my husband caused you earlier. He might blame you, but he's the one who looked like a fool."

Daniel placed his plate down and walked up close to her. Strands from his ponytail hung around his face, glinting gold in the lantern light.

"I had meant to thank you for standing up for me, earlier. It was the nicest thing anyone has done for me in a very long time. Well, actually, you have done many nice things for me. When Brandt blows his stack, I only know how to retreat or risk getting into more trouble. I swear sometimes he welcomes the challenge to prove how tough he is."

"He didn't hurt you, did he?"

She wasn't sure what look crossed his face, but he continued talking before she could ask.

"Nothing to worry yourself over. In any case, after you left, he was busy mumbling about you and your place in the house, he forgot about why he was angry until we got to the house. It was only then he decided I'd go without food."

She opened her mouth to speak but made the mistake of looking into his eyes instead. Hazel eyes with flecks of deep green. They projected a warmth and gentleness back at her. He was close; heat radiated from his body and beckoned her into it. His fingers trailed along her dress, tracing the satin ribbon inlayed along the fabric. He pressed his hand to her chest and smiled.

"Your heart is beating fast."

"Yes, I know." Her voice echoed what was in her mind in barely a whisper.

"Is it because of me?"

She nodded her head. Her pulse raced.

"Is it because you want me to kiss you?"

The words wouldn't come. Her yearning to feel his lips on hers was painful. A tear loosened from the corner of her eye and slid down her burning hot cheek.

"How about I answer for you?"

He took half a step forward and touched her shoulder. Tingles raced through her body, making it difficult for her to swallow. She should stop him from going any farther, but she didn't want to. His arms swept around her waist and pulled her closer. Her body melted into his without any choice on her part. His nose brushed against hers and she waited to feel his lips. Goose bumps spiraled along her body and she gasped as they connected. Any resistance had failed and she fused herself to him, pressing her lips against his, tasting his saltiness with a hint of rosemary and parsnip.

The kiss felt as sweet as any fantasy she could ever conjure up. Tongues collided, bringing a rush of heat to her insides. She pressed her body as far into him as she could get, her breasts bunched tight beneath her dress. His hands moved along her back, resting at the nape of her neck. With eyes closed, she let the moment take her away, in case it were a dream. His hands loosened from around her and he stepped back. It took a moment to regain her balance and for her mind to register what had happened. Immediately her fingers went to her lips, outlining where his had been stained against hers.

"Was I wrong to kiss you?"

She had no reason to think about it or hesitate. "No. I wanted it."

Before Daniel had time to say more, she let out a squeal and dove at his chest, nearly knocking him over. Instinctively he looked around her, his embrace tight and protective.

"What is it? What frightened you?"

Her whole body shook. "I saw something crawl across the floor. I think it might have been a mouse."

His booming laughter echoed inside the barn.

"Ah! Brill is my pet mouse. It looks like he has come to introduce himself to you."

Evelynn pulled back and narrowed her eyes. "Brill? You named a mouse?"

"Yes. I've made myself a companion. It gets kind of lonely in here, and there are many nights I find it hard to sleep. My mind is hard to quiet. One night I met Brill and fed him a few crumbs. Now we're great pals. It might be a little more one-sided than I'd care to admit, but what can you do. Would you like to meet him?"

She realized she was still nestled close in his arms and took a step back. Nervously she straightened her dress. "Well I...I'm not sure. Mice aren't exactly my cup of tea."

"Oh you'll like him. Nice disposition for a mouse. Give me a minute and I'll introduce you properly."

He bent down and looked about the floor, calling out Brill's name several times. In the far corner she made out the tiny form and watched as Daniel pressed his hand down to the floor. The little mouse scurried over quickly making a series of squeaks along the way. He carried it over to the plate of food and pulled off a small piece of biscuit, laying it on his hand.

"A little food tends to put him in a more social mood. You can touch him—if you like. He won't bite you, I promise."

She scrunched up her nose. It had nibbled up the crumb in only a few bites. Slowly she raised her hand and let it hover above Brill's head. "You're sure?"

"I promise. Brill and I know how to treat a lady. Go ahead."

Evelynn had to admit the little guy was cute, in its own mousy way. She stroked its head and started to giggle. "I never thought I'd pet a mouse."

"It's good to try new things."

"I guess I'm always afraid to get hurt. When I try new things, I mean. I feel safe around you, though."

Why was her mouth running away from her? Her loose tongue was going to get her into trouble if she wasn't careful.

His smile was genuine and helped her to relax.

"I'm glad. I wouldn't let anything or anyone hurt you."

She wanted to ask if he meant Brandt, but it didn't feel right. Daniel squatted down to lower the mouse back to the floor. Realizing she had overstayed, Evelynn started to make her way out.

"I must go."

"No need to rush off."

"I've stayed far too long as it is. I'll let you finish your meal. It's probably cold by now."

"Since you've been in here, I'd say everything has heated up."

A steady rise of warmth coated her face. He was such a charmer. A voice inside said she needed to leave immediately or risk consequences.

She turned without saying another word and fled from the barn, running to the back of her house where she silently relived the moment of the kiss they had shared. Evelynn paced along the flowerbeds, her fingertips passing along the petals. Should Brandt have walked in on them at any time, she would have been whipped, not to mention Daniel. Never before had she betrayed her husband, and it felt wrong on many levels.

Except for one. Wasn't she entitled to experience love the way it was meant to be? Would love be what it had always been, something slightly out of reach. It had come close, and she yearned for it, but it wasn't hers to take. Not while she was stuck married to a man who for the most part didn't even know she existed.

Her duties as a wife weren't much different than a servant. Greet him at the door, partake in idle chatter, be sure his clothes were laid out on the bed, and a body to clutch in the night. Their lovemaking amounted to nothing more than a few pecks on her cheek and a small procession of thrusts between her thighs only a few times in the beginning. She found pretending in bed wasn't for her. Passion was missing and her heart wasn't in it.

Her thoughts switched between her displeasure at Brandt and her desire for Daniel. Both were wrong on many levels. Complete opposites. She wanted to run from one and run to the other. Why was she like this?

She was not normally a selfish woman, but the years of being selfless were starting to build up. Where was the guilt and shame she should be feeling? Would it come when she saw Brandt's face? The tears weren't of sorrow, but of joy and release. Daniel's kiss was an awakening to the emotions she had locked up and stored away. All the stories her mother had told to her about the love between a man and woman came into play again. It did exist. There was such an emotion. She'd never experienced those things or understood what they meant, until now.

She had no idea how late it was, but she went back into the house and quietly closed the door. Turning, she

Ann Cory

ran straight into Brandt. There was the guilt. Her face and ears burned.

"Bess said you went up to lie down."

"I-I was on my way but decided to take a moment and get some fresh air. The nights are much cooler than usual for May."

"I'd say you were out there for a good chunk of time."

"Was I? Busy with thoughts I guess. Were you worried?"

She hoped he would say yes. He should be. Her husband should be greatly concerned that she was considering leaving him for another man. But he shook his head and put a rigid arm around her. Evelynn struggled to not push him away. He was trying, in his own way. She would give him a little credit. Only he was trying too late.

"I don't like to dine alone. Ruins my appetite. Tomorrow night let us try to work harder at getting along."

She looked up at him. His face was set in its usual grim expression. Did he mean it or was he mouthing the words?

"I will try."

"I'm exhausted and need sleep. Will you be up soon?"

"Yes. I won't be much longer."

"All right. Good night."

An awkward smile crossed his face and she mustered up her strength to smile in return. He walked up the stairs, slow, as if weights hung on the soles of his feet. Now wasn't the time for him to try and be different. Things were confusing enough as it was. What would have happened had he caught her kissing his apprentice? Waves of nausea crashed in her stomach at the thought. Would he react out of jealousy or would he react out of the dishonor she would bring to him? She feared more for Daniel's safety than her own.

Evelynn hugged her arms around her body and started up the stairs. It didn't matter what Brandt would do. She couldn't be with Daniel in the same way ever again. She'd gotten lost in the moment and now it was time to be the dutiful wife. But not in her dreams. Tonight she would see where her fantasies would take her. At least in her dreams she would let him go as far as he wanted.

Chapter Twelve

Daniel picked at the food, wishing he were hungrier for it. What he hungered for most was Evelynn's company. The taste of her lips against his made his whole body yearn for more. Oh how he'd wished to know the way her body felt tucked safely against his, and for a brief moment, the wish had been granted. His skin ached to feel hers pressed against his, for his fingers to travel among the strands of her mahogany hair and lose himself in its sweet scent. The rest of the evening would be torture as he relived the moment in his mind.

He forced himself to eat up the meat and potatoes, leaving the biscuits for Brill. As if he'd read his thoughts, the little mouse squeaked a greeting as it crawled back in.

"I have to hand it to you. Your timing is impeccable. You've got a good nose. If I didn't know any better, I'd say you were watching from the corner, waiting for your cue."

He carefully pulled off his shirt and lay down on the mattress on his stomach. It had taken everything in him to act as though he wasn't in pain. Had she seen the shape his back was in, she would have been furious and probably overreacted. Her visit had taken away the sting of the belt and healed his wounds, but now the pain was fierce. Because of her, he would stay and endure whatever torture he had to. All this time he had longed to find out what she felt for him, wondering if it was only in his head. The casual glances. Prolonged conversations. They'd held some validity to them. Tonight she had shown her feelings were mutual.

When she mentioned the situation with Brandt it had been without emotion or tenderness, as if they were words she'd recited to herself often. She had expressed herself with ease, trusting him, opening her heart to him without worry of his reactions or judgment. It meant the world to him. While he could have tested how far she was willing to go with him, it was a risk he wasn't ready to take.

He was raised a gentleman and wouldn't let his feelings get the upper hand. But the next time...he wouldn't pull away, or let her leave. The next time, he would taste more than her lips.

Chapter Thirteen

Evelynn woke up in time to hear Brandt leaving out the door. He would probably be angry she hadn't gotten up with him, but she hardly cared. Lazily she stretched in bed, letting the stray fingers of sleep let go of her. Her dreams had been arousing and she kept waking up, hoping to turn and see Daniel lying beside her instead of the man who dared to call himself her husband.

The young apprentice had stirred her with his appearance from the moment he first came in the house. In the beginning, she chalked it up to his charm and how his boyish qualities were refreshing in the somber house. It wasn't long before she came to realize how little she and her husband communicated. She'd known it before, deep inside, but the presence of someone else made it painfully clear.

Daniel would talk contently for hours, when Brandt let him, and share with them about his family, though he always got choked up when he started to talk about his sister. She kept meaning to ask him about her, but feared he would think her insensitive. His past intrigued her because she knew little about it.

The sound of Bess washing dishes reminded her about the sewing lessons she'd promised. It would do both of them some good if she could take her mind off the disappointments in her life and be productive. With the events of the evening still fresh in her mind, she twirled herself across the floor and picked up the fabric she'd bought. She brushed off the dirt from the dress material and set it on the bed. When she picked up the lace she felt the fury rise in her stomach. There was no way she would be able to wash the smudges from the detailed etchings sewn along the lace.

Evelynn threw it to the floor and tore off her dressing gown. She glanced through her closet and picked out an elegant blue dress with ribbons and did her hair up nice. As she made her way down the stairs, she caught a whiff of bacon sizzling and she heard her stomach grumble.

"Smells delicious."

"Thank you, ma'am. Care for any eggs this morning? You didn't have dinner last night so I figure you to be ravenous."

"No, I'll be fine with tea, fruit, and a couple pieces of bacon. I will need to make another trip into town to buy a new yard of lace. When I return, we can start our first lesson. I will do my best to make it fun. I've never taught anyone to sew before, but my mother taught me and I had a grand time learning."

"I'm looking forward to it, ma'am."

Evelynn sat at the table and sipped her tea, playing with the edge of the tablecloth.

"Tell me, how was my husband's mood this morning?"

"The usual, not much to say. It was quiet in here. Too quiet for me. Makes the rattle of the dishes even louder. I missed Daniel's company this morning. He always livens things up."

"Yes, I feel the same. I hope the food I brought him last night will last him until dinner tonight. As much as I wanted to get up early and sneak some bread out to him, I was too worried Brandt would have a fit. I'm hoping he cooled off and things will be back to normal."

Evelynn nibbled on her crispy bacon and pushed around the fruit. She thought about Brandt and the way he'd spoken to her. Banning her from the blacksmith shop was too irrational for words. He wanted to make it seem like he wasn't in the wrong, but she wasn't going to let him. She was going back. Not to defy her husband, but to make a point. There was no way she was going to let him keep winning the fights. If he truly respected her, he wouldn't have a problem with her showing up.

"Bess, I won't be long."

"You be careful, ma'am, I heard what the master said about you not being allowed..."

Evelynn put her hand up and shook her head. "Please, don't call him that. Brandt is only a master in his mind. He's got too many people fooled and it's time he got a taste of his own medicine. I don't think anything will come of this necessarily, but it's worth a try."

"You're a defiant woman, Mrs. Whitling. I look up to you."

"I'm a very poor role model. I've done nothing right in my life to warrant such a positive title. I would rather you learned from my mistakes than anything."

"You are much too hard on yourself. I see with my own two eyes how kind you are and the way you treat people. You stand up for yourself and people do respect you. For as much as your husband wants to rule the roost, you are still stronger than he could ever hope to be. I think he gets his strength from you."

Evelynn thought about the Bess' words for a few moments, letting them all digest. She'd never considered how Bess saw her.

"I'm not sure if that's the case. Okay, I'll be back shortly. I've left the dress pattern on my bed if you'd like to take a look at it. I promise it looks harder than it is."

"Yes, ma'am. I must admit I am curious."

Evelynn opened the door and was disappointed to see it raining. The ground looked like it was made of water and was turning everything to mud. She refused to let it change her plans and grabbed a parasol to shield her from the drops. This time she took a different route into town, poking her head inside the window of the boot and harness shop. She loved boots in all different styles and colors. Brandt thought she had more than enough pairs, but this time she was looking at a pair of boots for Daniel. His were horribly worn. She noticed a pair on the counter with good sturdy hard-soles on them, but didn't know what size he took. If she got the chance, she would check and take some of her secret money to purchase them.

She slowly strolled under the covered bridge and passed by the apothecary, general store, sawmill, smoke house, and the dry good's store. The wind blew a little stronger, giving her a chill she couldn't seem to shake.

On her way to the blacksmith's shop, she passed by Grace and Dorothy. The bacon immediately did flip-flops in her stomach. She should have known they would be out trying to stick their noses where they didn't belong. Today she would appease them by acting as though nothing had happened.

"Afternoon, ladies," she called, swinging the bell-shape skirt of her dress around.

Grace gave her a strange stare.

"Is there something wrong? Have I done something to upset you?"

The woman squinted and looked her up and down. "No."

"Why are you both looking at me in such a strange fashion?"

"Dorothy and I were discussing your little outburst yesterday. Quite a public display. Never seen anything like it before."

"To be honest, I've completely put it out of my mind. It's a new day, why rehash the past?"

Grace exchanged glances with her friend. "I don't know. We are well aware you and Brandt have a unique relationship, but bringing it out into public...it wasn't a proper thing for a lady to do."

All ready Evelynn was bored with the charade. They weren't about to let it go. "Tell me, how exactly does it affect either one of you?"

She felt herself getting mad and tried to think of pleasant things.

"It's not how it affected us, but we were subjected to it. You are the wife of a blacksmith and it's your role in the community to uphold certain standards."

"I see. And which standards are these? It seems strange to me how two gossiping spinsters wouldn't know very much about any kind of standards."

Dorothy sneered. "I beg your pardon."

Evelynn couldn't quiet her tongue. "I suppose I should apologize because you were forced to listen to our scuffle, but it doesn't change the fact it happened, now does it? If it bothered you, why did you stick around to listen to it? When two people live under the same roof they are bound to find fault with one another, as well as having a difference in opinion."

"Yes. We are well aware of other couples having disagreements, but they do it within the walls of their home."

"My husband spends more time at his workplace than at home. I spoke to him where it was most convenient at the time. I wish I could stand around and talk about this all day, but I have other things to do. If you have a problem with my being open and direct about things, I am very sorry. Unlike the domesticated women who are afraid of their husbands, I'm not afraid to speak my mind."

Frustrated and infuriated, she clomped all the way to Judy's shop. The nerve of those two! She couldn't stand people who made it their business to talk about others. She didn't feel she belonged in this town. When she went inside the shop, only a few people stood around the counter. From the way they stared, it appeared they had all heard about the big shouting match.

Timidly she asked, "Is Judy here?"

An elderly woman walked from behind the counter and smiled. "She won't be in until later, dear. May I help you with something?"

Evelynn looked around. What had she come in for again? All eyes were on her and it was making her uncomfortable.

"No. I'll drop in tomorrow. Thank you."

When she stepped out, the air had changed. The skies had turned a deep charcoal gray and brought a wind that chilled her bones. A raindrop splattered against her cheek. Of all the days to forget to wear a coat. Evelynn decided against her talk with Brandt and headed for home as fast as she could.

Chapter Fourteen

Brandt burst open the barn doors and hollered for Daniel to get up.

"It's nothing but mud on the ground. I figure we better get an early start."

Daniel put on his pants and eased the shirt over his head.

"Here. Brought you a muffin and some apples. Might as well eat something. Can't afford for you to get sick."

"Thanks." He laced up his boots and grabbed a wide-brimmed hat.

"Let's get going. The tools aren't going to fix themselves. Got anything you want to say to me?"

He clenched his jaw. "No. Why?"

"I see. I figured you would have enough sense to prattle out an apology. But I guess not."

"I refuse to apologize for something I didn't do."

"Whatever. We'll sort this out later."

Outside, the ground was puddle after puddle, making their walk to the forge slick.

Brandt mumbled the whole way in. "Rained all night. I hate the rain. Means I'll get a bunch of wagon wheels in."

"I would think you'd welcome the chance to make more money."

"I don't have time to waste mending wheels. They are as bad as horseshoes. I hate those worse. Now get a move on, boy. Time's a wasting with your incessant chatter."

Daniel hadn't slept well after Evelynn left. A few moments of sweet dreams about her were all he got. Once the rain started up, it clanged noisily against the roof, and his back kept him twisting in pain. Each step was a reminder of how much he loathed the man.

As he opened up the doors to the shop, he felt one of the wounds open up. He bit his lip to keep from shouting. He didn't want to give his employer the satisfaction. Sweat beaded on his forehead as the shirt scraped against the welts. Brandt didn't seem to care much; he was too busy moving around a pile of vises.

"Well, what do we have here? Would you look at what I found? The blasted anvil."

Daniel glared. "Should have known you had it hidden all this time."

"Me? Why would I do something so stupid? I was looking for it yesterday, same as you."

He wasn't falling for his childish prank. "You knew where not to look."

"Is there something you want to say to me?"

"No."

"Good. Get the fire going and do some work around here."

Daniel kept trying to work but the discomfort was a distraction. When he reached for something the shirt got caught on the edge of his sores and stung until his eyes watered. The more he moved around the more he began to sweat and it didn't help matters. He threw down a hammer and stood with his hands on his hips.

When he turned, Brandt was eyeing him, a large grin on his grimy face. "Looks like you're in some pain."

"Yes, as a matter of fact, I am."

"Sorry."

"No, you aren't," Daniel sneered.

"You don't believe me?"

"No. You deliberately hid the anvil to give you an excuse to beat me with your belt."

"You don't make any sense. Tell you what, though. I'll give you an easy job for the next hour." Brandt took out an order sheet from his back pocket and handed it over to him. "I need you to take this order to the tanner's and afterwards drop off the tools we fixed yesterday to Harris."

"Where would I find Harris today?"

"The dam. He's the new guy in charge. Can't figure out why, but no one asked for my opinion."

"Okay."

"Don't take too long. There's a lot of work to do."

"Yes, sir." More like slave driver, he wanted to say.

He grabbed the armful of tools from the back corner and headed off to the South Fork Dam. The clouds in the sky had turned black and the rain was coming down even harder. Daniel tried to run but the feel of his wet shirt against the open wounds made it too difficult. At the site, he recognized the man he was looking for standing under a tree to stay dry.

"Harris, right?"

"Yes."

He walked up and thrust out his hand. "Daniel McCray. I'm..."

"Ahh. The apprentice to that hard-nosed blacksmith."

"Yes, sir, you are correct."

The man shook his hand in return and frowned. "My condolences. You couldn't pay me enough to work with him. He's nothing but an old ogre."

"Yes, well, word never got to Virginia about him or I would have tried my luck elsewhere. I had to find out the hard way, I guess."

"Whatcha got there for me?"

Daniel propelled the bundle of tools toward the man and brushed his hands off on the legs of his trousers. "All the tools you sent over are fixed up."

"Good. Good. I suspect you did most of the work?"

"Well..."

"Oh, go on. You can tell me. I'm not a fan of Mr. Brandt Whitling."

He couldn't help but laugh at the quirky man. "Seeing as how you put it that way, yes."

"I am sure they are all fixed right as rain."

"Speaking of rain...it looks like we've got us another storm coming. This rain doesn't plan to lighten up any time soon. I can feel it in my bones."

"Storm's coming out of Nebraska and Kansas, I'm afraid. Heading east the whole way. It's been bad over there. We're expected to have one of the worst rains in a long time."

"South Fork Dam going to hold up against it?"

He watched Harris screw up his face in thought. "I have my concerns."

"What are you planning to do about those concerns?"

"I worry about Stony Creek. Because of its position, it could cause flooding. Beyond that, we don't have a discharge pipe. There's no way to regulate the dam or help with water reduction."

"Doesn't sound good."

"You don't even know the half of it. The last repairs caused a major leak and it has been cutting into the new embankment."

"Have you told anybody about all of this?"

"Of course! Seems no one wants to put out their money to see it gets done right. We're in for trouble if the rains keep on."

Daniel switched his weight to his other foot. "How bad?"

"Don't know. I expect we'll make it through like we always do."

"But you aren't sure."

Harris ran a hand through his mass of curly hair and straightened his glasses. "Can't be too sure of anything."

"I don't envy the level of your responsibility for this. Let's hope the storm moves through quickly."

"The men and I will be checking out everything off and on through the night. Thank you for the tools."

"No problem."

Daniel watched Harris run over to a group of men all standing around, shouting at one another. He hadn't realized what a sore subject the dam was. Everywhere he went folks were talking about it. He made a brief stop at the tanner's and gave Louis the work order. The walk back was slow going with his boots getting stuck in the mud every few steps. A new wave of worry had ebbed within him. While he was only a houseguest and apprentice, he'd made Pennsylvania his home, leaving behind old ghosts in Virginia.

There was Evelynn to consider. This was her only home. He worried what would happen if the flooding got too bad and tore through the town. He'd lost one person who meant something to him. He didn't want to go through it again.

Chapter Fifteen

As Daniel headed back to the shop, he was surprised to see Evelynn. Her face was set in a scowl but she still looked beautiful in his eyes. In his mind he called out to her, but he didn't want to risk someone overhearing and going to Brandt about it. As if she'd heard him, her head turned. She changed direction and came at him, lowering her parasol to the ground.

"What are you doing here?"

"I was sent to run errands. What brings you out during such unsavory conditions?"

"My temper, I'm afraid. I had every intention of giving Brandt a piece of my mind but people and their ignorance delayed me. It was turning into a horrid day, until I saw you."

The way the rain fell against her face was beautiful. Liquid kisses.

"Daniel, I don't know how much more I can take of this place, my husband, any of it. I feel like I'm going mad. My mind is everywhere and I feel trapped, like someone has hold of my lungs with a vise and won't let go. Every day I feel it being tightened."

"I understand. I've felt the same way. You aren't going mad, I promise."

She rushed at him and gripped his shoulders, her fingers refusing to let go.

"I want you to take me somewhere. Right now. Take me away from here, even if it's only for a few minutes. I need it."

At first he didn't understand. Brandt would be expecting him back at any minute, and he was in enough trouble as it was. He looked around, relieved no one was watching. If word got back...he didn't even want to think those thoughts.

"I only need a few minutes of your time. Please."

"Where do you want to go?"

She grabbed his arm and pulled him behind a large tree.

"Remember the kiss we shared? I've thought of nothing else. You took me to the moon with those lips. Imagine where we could go if you did more."

He placed his fingers to her chin and raised her face up to him.

"Such beautiful lips. The kind I could kiss for days."

"Take me away, please."

Her breathy whispers made it impossible to resist. He pressed his lips to hers, groping at her with his mouth and tongue. She pushed him against the trunk of the tree and slid her hand inside his shirt. The bark of the tree bit into his back, mangling it up even more, but he wouldn't let it interrupt the moment. God she was all hands and lips, digging her nails into him one minute and caressing him gently the next. The savagery only aroused him further and he couldn't make himself stop.

He pulled her close and gathered her dress and petticoats in his hands, yards of fabric and lace, pulling the material high enough to get his fingers where he wanted them most.

"Oh God Daniel. I need this. More than you know."

She kissed at his neck and face, pecking away at him with determined ferocity. Her rough hands knocked his hat from his head, landing on the ground beside them.

He felt his cock thicken inside his trousers, seeking out her feminine heat. The rain came down harder, lashing at them. He could see it. He knew it existed. But he couldn't feel it. His heart was racing. What if someone saw? Anyone could pass by and catch them. They would be sure to notify Brandt and he would hunt him down. He didn't dare look. All he wanted to see was her.

"I want you, Daniel McCray."

"And I you. I have since the day we met."

She slipped her hands into his trousers and palmed him with her smooth skin. If only he could pin her down and thrust his cock between her thighs, but this wasn't the time or place. He prayed there would be such a time. His growing need for her, to consume her, take her in every way possible was bigger than he was. He rested his hand against her belly and slowly draped his fingers down, caught off guard by the heat generating from her.

The smell of her arousal crept into his nose and tweaked his senses. He didn't want to be a gentleman. He wanted to take her like an animal.

"Feel me. Feel the devotion I have for you."

She needn't ask a second time. Inside the forbidden zone that had beckoned to him from his most ethereal of dreams, he found his true home. His fingers drank from her juices, spiraling around and sweeping in patterns he wished to mimic with his cock. Evelynn squirmed in his arms, her body tight against him. The ripened peaks of her breasts caressed his chest, prodding at him with a will of their own. As he opened her up, she stroked him hard. Time wasn't on their side and they both longed for the release together, one way or another.

He fondled her wet labia fast, keeping up with the unyielding way in which she rubbed at him. The shortness of her breath let him know she was close. He wouldn't let her go without giving her the satisfaction she sought.

His lips sought out her earlobe and he whispered to her, in the hopes of helping her over the edge.

"My darling, I cannot wait to have you in private, all of you with your full naked body bent over my bed, my lips kissing the curvature of your womanly form. To not have you as a silhouette in an altered state of consciousness, but to truly experience the real you."

She moaned and sighed into his neck, her body losing balance as she neared the breaking point. He grinded against her until he finally met his needs as well. A devilish smile crept on her face. She was pleased with herself for getting her way. The smile faded as he upped the price and circled his thumb around her clit with such intensity her eyes rolled up in the back of her head, her eyelids fluttering like wings of a butterfly.

"Now, oh God, now I…" Her whispered pleas cut off as she threw back her head and let out a barreled cry. His fingers welcomed the warmth and stroked her slower and slower until her shaking subsided. She leaned into him, resting her head on his chest. His legs were weak holding them both up.

As the orgasm subsided the agony of his back against the bark of the tree nearly made him pass out. He couldn't let her know, though, and gripped her tighter.

"Did you like where I took you?"

"Yes, very much." Even her voice quivered. Her beautiful blue eyes batted at him and stared at him with a bounty of love. It wasn't fair to want a woman he couldn't have. A woman who belonged to a man he feared and loathed.

Daniel let go of her dress and let it rest back around her ankles. He rested his cheek against her forehead.

"I should go. I don't want to, but I must."

She nodded. "I know."

"Before I do, may I have one more kiss?"

"Of course."

This time the kiss was soft and languid. Neither wanted their lips to part, knowing the goodbye was inevitable.

She slipped from his grasp and walked away.

"Every bit a lady," he said as he watched her form get smaller in the distance.

Chapter Sixteen

He tucked in his shirt and fixed his trousers. It would be a long shot but he hoped Brandt wouldn't recognize the honeysuckle smell of Evelynn on his clothes. He reached down and grabbed his hat, knocking a puddle of water from the rim off against his thigh. With a heavy sigh, he headed for the forge.

Daniel paused a moment outside of the entrance to gather his wits about him. He wouldn't miss this place. It wasn't his calling. There were plenty of skills he had to serve him well in other occupations. He stepped into the darkness of the forge and stood in front of the fire to dry. The thoughts of the destruction of a flood drifted back on his mind and a new stream of adrenaline flowed.

"Brandt. Can I talk to you a minute?"

"Something wrong with the order?"

"No. I wanted to ask you a few questions."

Brandt gave him a gruff look and set his anvil down. "What is it? Make it quick. You've wasted enough time. There's a lot of work to be done here. You sure took your time."

"I only stopped once to talk with Harris. Seems there is an even bigger concern about the dam. The rumors have been circulating for days. The oncoming storm could cause a serious flood. Enough to wash this whole town right away."

Brandt snorted. "It's not the first time talk of a flood has happened around here. People are convinced the dam was built improperly, and the gossip has spread like wildfire. You mind what you're supposed to be doing here. There's nothing to be concerned about."

"Suppose the dam did break. You realize not a single house could withstand the rushing torrent of water?"

"My home would."

"Are you sure?"

"It was built tall and the framework is sturdy. If anything the first floor would suffer damage, but the top floor wouldn't be touched."

"No doubts?"

"Nope."

"Is it built strong enough to keep Evelynn safe?"

Brandt whipped around, a red-hot piece of iron in his hand. "Mrs. Whitling, to you. Do not disrespect my wife again or I'll take this anvil and give you a crack to your skull."

The thought sent shivers up Daniel's spine.

"Yes, sir, my apologies. Your wife. Will she be safe and protected in case of a natural disaster?"

"I built both my house and the boarding house with my own two hands. They are both strong structures."

"Harris said this storm is supposed to be the biggest one yet."

Brandt glared. "Johnstown has weathered its fair share of storms. The creeks are always overflowing after a hard rain. Life will go on as it always does. Are you done with the questions?"

"I'm concerned. About Bess too. You are the only family I have now. I worry about what happens. To all of you."

"Especially my wife, though. Right?"

Daniel bit his tongue. If he lied, it would show on his face. As much as he wanted to tell him he'd been with his wife, he couldn't dishonor Evelynn. She had suffered enough over the years and she trusted him to keep their union a secret. Brandt didn't give him a chance to answer.

"Enough nonsense. The dam will hold. Unless you're some expert dam builder, I don't want to hear you spouting anything more about it. You've only lived here a couple of years and you haven't seen how quickly the town recovers from a small amount of flooding."

"I'm not an expert. I'm observant."

Brandt grabbed him roughly by the shoulders and shook him. "Don't think I'm not observant in the way you look at my wife at the dinner table. I've seen you watch the way she eats. I know the look in another man's eyes when he sees something he likes. She's a beautiful woman, and she belongs to me."

"I'm well aware, sir. But she shouldn't be your possession."

"I forbid you to look at her in any way I deem improper. You hear me, boy? I'll have you out of the house so fast you won't know what hit you. She may have talked me into letting you have dinner with us, but I'll be damned if I put up with indecency."

Daniel tried to keep his tone light. "I think you're making too much of what is simply my being kind to her. You're mistaking my sensitive words and compliments for something illicit. I have been nothing less than a gentleman."

"The only gentleman welcome in my house is me. Whether she considers me to be one or not is not for me to say. Now. If you'd like to apologize properly, I will be easier on you."

"Go to hell!"

Brandt grabbed him by his ponytail and flung him to the ground. In seconds he was thrashing his back with a rope. The twine only made his previous beating harder to bear.

"Since you seem to be lacking respect, I will teach you some. No one will care if you left tomorrow. If you never work another day here as an apprentice, I wouldn't lose a minute of sleep over it. You've been a thorn in my side since day one. I should have known by your scrawny size you'd never amount to anything."

"Stop!" Daniel tried to pull himself up but Brandt pinned him down with the heel of his boot.

"Let me up! I haven't done anything wrong."

He tried again to get up and was unsuccessful.

Brandt lifted his foot and kicked him in the sides with brute force, sending him into a pile of loose bricks.

"What the hell is the matter with you?"

Daniel clambered to his feet as fast as he could, coughing and wheezing. With his fist closed tight, he rammed it into the blacksmith's stomach.

"You think you can beat me? You are finished. As of close of business today. Our working relationship has come to an end."

"I've done nothing wrong. These accusations you spout are things made up in your head, fueled by your guilt and conscience. You will get no more work out of me today. I am leaving!"

"You don't go unless I give the word. I expect a full day's work."

He could see the fire in Brandt's eyes and knew if he stayed, he might not walk out alive. This wasn't about who had control, who was the strongest, or being a man. It had everything to do with the love of one woman. Daniel headed out into the rain and ran as fast as he could to the safety of the barn, never once looking back. His pants and hose were splattered with mud and his boots sunk hard into the ground. By the time he got to the barn, he was exhausted and out of breath. He pushed open the doors and stared at the place he'd called home for two years.

ঞ ঞ ঞ

Evelynn floated on air the whole way home. Not even the rain could dampen her spirits. Her legs were strengthened by the power charging through her entire body. All the years of wondering what it would feel like to hold his cock in her hands and now she knew. With a single touch, she was able to tap into his inner needs. Surges of energy sparked each step through the muddied ground. Bypassing puddle after puddle she skipped along, uncaring how much dirt tread along the hem of her dress.

When she reached her home, she opened the door and closed it fast behind her. Evelynn, leaned against its sturdy weight to keep her balance. To know a man could make her feel more like a woman replenished the cup of hope that emptied every night. Daniel could save her with a look, a touch, a kiss.

As Bess rounded the corner, Evelynn pulled herself together and hung up the parasol. Drenched like her, it left a puddle of raindrops on the floor.

"Are you all right, Mrs. Whitling? Your cheeks are flushed. Shall I draw you a bath?"

"A bath would be lovely. Thank you."

Evelynn noticed the earlier twinkle in the maid's eyes had left. A wave of guilt hit her. She rushed toward Bess and clasped her hands.

"Wait, Bess. I haven't forgotten our sewing lesson. Since Judy wasn't in today, I couldn't buy more lace. I feel terrible to have built up your excitement. I ran into...a distraction on my way home."

"I understand, Mrs. Whitling. I take no offense."

"I am pleased to hear it. Let us make a definite plan tomorrow. I will worry about the lace at another time."

"I am excited to learn. You spoke with him?"

Evelynn's body shuddered at the thought of Daniel's words whispered in her ears. "Hmm? Who?"

"Mr. Whitling, of course."

"Right, of course. My husband. No, after I left Judy's I realized whatever I wanted to say could wait. The ground is damp and makes it difficult to walk on. I will speak with him this evening after supper. Goodness knows he throws a fit when I try and talk beforehand."

"Will Daniel be joining us this evening?"

"I would certainly hope so. I can't imagine Brandt making him go another night without food. I won't allow it."

"I will make a special meal for the young apprentice."

"I look forward to it."

She bent over and started to undo her boots.

"If you are done with me, ma'am, I will start on your bath."

"Sounds heavenly, Bess. Thank you. For everything."

Chapter Seventeen

Evelynn had enjoyed her luxurious soak in the warm water, tracing her hands along all the places Daniel had touched her. She'd taken a big risk by displaying her needs for Daniel in public. It was fortunate no one had caught them. Where the strength came from, she didn't know, but she wasn't sorry. Their brief time together was further proof of how she could no longer stay confined in the walls of a loveless marriage. Something had to give. The desire to wait for her husband to change was now a thing of the past.

A new calm had settled over her, cleansing away the anxious sensations that all too often plagued her mind. She was still restless, but not with the same intensity. Her head was clear, thoughts more focused. Love had made her whole and she couldn't continue to live without it. She needed the newfound energy to explore the rest of her future. Contentedly she sighed and finished making herself look nice. By the time she arrived downstairs, Bess was finishing up dinner. It would be difficult to pretend her rendezvous with Daniel didn't happen, but she would find a way.

Her peace of mind changed when Brandt walked in the door. Alone. She bit her tongue to keep from harping at him with a thousand questions. She would wait for him to sit at the table and see if he would willingly explain.

As Bess brought in several platters of food, Evelynn sat at the table, her hands clenched in tight fists on the tabletop.

"Are you going to sit there and not say anything?

"I don't need to explain myself to you."

"I refuse to believe Daniel chose to not dine with us yet again. He enjoys Bess' cooking far too much."

"He showed disrespect to me and I punished him."

"You are nothing but a hateful monster. He doesn't deserve to go hungry."

"Doesn't make much difference to me what you think about it. Would you raise this much fuss if I didn't show up for supper?"

She wasn't going to give him the satisfaction by answering how he wanted. "I don't know why you bother coming home as it is. Whether you are here or not, I feel as though I am alone. At least Daniel brings some warmth into this cold house."

He tried intimidating her with his stare but she rose to the challenge and met his gaze. If she could steal away without being seen, she would bring Daniel some food again. And a biscuit for Brill.

Evelynn watched her husband pile slabs of meat onto his plate and proceed to attack his food as if it were still alive. He chewed roughly and looked up at her.

"Are you going to eat or sit there and watch me?"

"I haven't decided yet. Might help if you explained to me what's going on. Why are you picking on the poor boy more than usual?"

"You know I don't like discussion at the dinner table. It's the only time I get any peace. One can't chew their food properly if they are expected to answer questions all the time."

"I see. You don't get any peace in your home. As opposed to spending time in your parlor and being asleep. It is no wonder I am lonely. You never have anything to say to me."

He clanged his eating utensils down and stared hard at her.

"You obviously have some things you'd like to talk about. I am done eating now. Please...enlighten me."

She didn't care for his tone, but she had his attention. "People go out of their way to do things for you, learn from you, but you never extend any kindness back. Why?"

He shrugged and tore at his biscuit.

"Hmm. Not interested in talking about yourself? All right. What is it you want from me? As a partner, a wife. I need to know."

"I want you to know your place."

Evelynn drummed her fingers against the table to try and keep her cool. "And what is my place?"

"Here, in the home where you belong."

"You want me to be the one who cooks and cleans for you, not Bess. I should work for you instead of making you spend your precious hard-earned money by paying someone else. Right?"

"Right. I had expectations when I married you and you haven't lived up to a single one."

"I see." She took a sip of tea and watched his eyebrows come together. "What's on your mind that has you in such a foul temper?"

"Nothing. Work. Matters I don't want to share with you."

"Aren't you in the least bit interested in what I would like from you. As my husband and partner. Or do you not care?"

"No. I do what I am supposed to do. Provide for you, take care of all the outside work, and make the money. If you want more, you will be disappointed."

Evelynn sat back in her chair and crossed her arms. "I have every right to want more, because what I have leaves me empty. I have been disappointed for the length of our marriage. Do you know why? You never look at me with kind eyes. You don't speak to me in a kind voice. I am treated about as well as any person who works for you."

"We started out okay in the beginning."

"Those times are all in your head. You saw what you wanted to see. It's all visuals to you."

"I saw an opportunity and took it. You didn't have to accept my proposal."

"I was young and inexperienced. I didn't know what I was getting into. If I could go back and change things, I would."

"You don't mean…"

"I think one of us needs to accept the truth here."

He leaned forward and clasped his hands together. "Are you saying you never loved me?"

"I don't think I did, Brandt. You were a way out of a situation. I was naïve at the time. I watched my father love my mother with every ounce of his being. They had a special bond."

"No two relationships are the same. I can't be someone I'm not."

Evelynn nodded her head. "Precisely. Neither can I. But it's what you expect of me. You believe everything I do or don't do reflects on you. It's a pressure I don't wish to have placed on me. You know nothing of love."

"You place too much emphasis on silly things. Do you think of nothing else but how to hurt me? I refuse to sit here and listen to my wife claim she doesn't love me!"

"They aren't words to me. Feelings have to be attached somewhere. I can't have children with someone I think of as a stranger. We can't change things if we never talk. You've been cold for a very long time. I've become numb inside. Even if you were to try and change now, it wouldn't work. We are two different people, with nothing in common."

"We are wasting our time here. You want me to let you go and run off with some other man where you can fulfill a fantasy you've built up in your mind?"

She sighed. Anything she said was being turned around and placed on her. "No. You aren't listening. I am here with you and trying to talk to you openly. You like to raise your voice and get angry so you can stomp away to your parlor and have the last word. There are a lot of things going on in my head too, but you don't care what they are."

"Would these things in your head half to do with Daniel?"

She swallowed down the truth. "No, of course not. Why would you ask?"

"A feeling."

"You have those?"

Brandt scooted back the chair and stood up. "I won't listen to you continue to make me look like the bad guy. Something is going on under my roof and I am putting a stop to it right now!"

"Do you even know what you are saying?"

Brandt gripped the edge of the table and shook it. "The both of you seem to care a lot about each other. If I ever catch you up to no good, I will whip him until you don't recognize him anymore."

The blood in her face drained out. She could see him doing it. "Does violence make you feel more like a man?"

He came up close to her face and pointed toward the stairs. "Get up to the bedroom and stay put."

Evelynn snorted. "What? You can't order me to my room. I'm not a child."

"No. You're my wife. You will show me some respect by doing what I tell you to do. Get upstairs or I'll pick up this table and break it into a million pieces. There won't be a need for anyone to have dinner in here. Trust me when I say that I will do it."

"Have you lost your mind?"

Evelynn was confused. What was all this about? This wasn't his usual stance in a fight. His body shook as he stared at her with eyes sharp enough to pierce her heart. It was too late. There was no question. A stranger stood before her, more of a stranger now than when he'd walked through the door. Something had distorted his usual frame of mind. The last piece of hope she had to reconcile their seven miserable years had blown out.

She stood and returned his gaze, her own fire brewing inside. "Fine, Brandt. I will go to bed. But I will not be made to feel like a prisoner here. If I choose to get up and take a walk, I will. If you lay an unkind hand on me, I will make you sorry for the rest of your life. I will tarnish your name and take everything you've got."

Evelynn turned and walked up the stairs. She would wait until he came up and fell asleep. When the time was right she would get up and sneak out of the house. She needed to see Daniel.

Chapter Eighteen

Brandt ascended the stairs and undressed, watching the way Evelynn slept. The moonlight fell against her face and made her appear like an angel. He sat on the edge of the bed and she stirred, her hands grasping the sheets with her fingers curled and tight.

"Yes. Take me again and again. Don't ever stop taking me."

He couldn't believe his ears. It was obvious the man she was crying out for wasn't him. The name didn't matter. It was clear the talk earlier had been her way of smoothing things over before she left him. A devious plan to make him look like a fool. If she wanted him to make things easier for her and force her to leave, she was in for a surprise. He wouldn't have it. Not in his house! He was the master here and no two-bit apprentice would steal his wife.

She continued to moan, her head rocking side to side. A film of perspiration coated her forehead. The way her voice sounded it was a sure sign she was in love with him. He recited her last words in his head. They didn't have anything in common. There was nothing left for them to do. He felt like he was giving up before he ever had the chance to do something about it. Letting her go would be the same as admitting defeat. He wasn't raised to take things lying down.

How could he have not taken the appropriate measures to keep this from happening? Ever since he'd brought the young man into his home, he'd had a slight concern that she would see all the qualities in him and compare the two of them. Of course he would lose. How could he compete against a man younger than he? Full of love and life? He'd tried to deplete Daniel's enthusiasm, but until recently he had been unsuccessful. Brandt knew he wasn't a good husband and lacked the mannerisms, gentlemanly behavior, and chiseled good looks. He hoped he made up for those with his intelligence and strength. According to his wife, he'd been wrong.

His temper was getting the better of him. He was getting more and more out of control every day. It disturbed him how much satisfaction he got out of beating Daniel with his belt. Lately he found himself ready to strike Evelynn. She was always baiting him and pushing him to the limit. Always going on about wanting freedom. While she was ten years younger, he hadn't realized how much the distance would show as they aged. She was far too fiery and outspoken for her own good and it made his blood boil. He didn't know who to blame more. His wife for having thoughts of another man while still married. Or Daniel for coming into their lives and giving her an idea of how good it could be with someone else.

To his knowledge, Daniel had only glanced at her around dinner, but he'd never seen them together. If he ever did, there would be hell to pay. This was his house, his land, and she was his wife. It was his duty and responsibility to fight for her to the death. Whoever's death should come from it, didn't much matter to him. The fight would be enough.

He closed his eyes and forced himself to fall asleep amid her restless sighs. Brandt couldn't be sure if he'd heard the floorboards squeak several minutes later, or he'd imagined it. When the sound stopped, he let go of his daunting day and surrendered to the night.

Chapter Nineteen

Daniel paced around the barn, doing his best to stave off the urge to tear the place apart, one wooden plank at a time. Adrenaline surged inside his body at such a fast rate it left him unsteady in his steps.

He didn't care that he was alone; it felt good to hear his voice. As if talking to his grandfather, he wrung his hands together tightly, looked up at the roof.

"I need to leave here! I cannot take this anymore. If you were still alive you'd tell me to run and not look back. I know with every ounce of my being that I am not a coward. This isn't the life I'd envisioned."

The anger continued to build. He threw the barn doors open and let the rain pelt at his face until he was drenched.

Any other time, he'd leave without a second thought. Without a stitch of clothing or money to his name. He'd done it before. But there was something...no, he needed to get real with himself, there was someone who made him stay. She didn't have to ask, he stayed willingly. Leaving Evelynn to her monster of a husband was not an option. His love for her grew stronger each day, and after their encounter, he was convinced there was more to her plea of him taking her away. She was looking to him to help her out of a situation she felt helpless in. What she was looking for, he could offer her. She wasn't looking for money or riches, but love in its purest form. He could give her it all. They needed to leave Johnstown together and find a new place to call their own. But how could he possibly run off with her while she was still a married woman? He was dreaming if he thought Brandt would let her go without a fight. Come the morning he would be asked to leave and his heart would break.

Daniel considered going back to Virginia and sending for her once he found a small place. The time apart would not sit right with him. She was a part of his life and he couldn't walk away.

The wind blew the doors shut and blew out the lantern. He didn't bother relighting it. Exhausted, he undressed and lay in bed. The rain battered the roof of the barn something fierce, trying to get in while he was trying to find a way out. It would be a long night.

Chapter Twenty

The sound of the barn doors tearing open startled Daniel from his half sleep. He looked and a flash of lightning illuminated the figure of a woman. Evelynn stood in the entrance, soaked, a long dressing gown clinging to her body like a second skin. He blinked several times and rubbed his eyes. It was similar to the dream he'd had the other night.

He wanted to tell her to come in or she'd catch her death, but he couldn't form the words. His lips felt glued to his teeth, his throat raw and achy. As if reading his mind, she came toward him.

"Brandt doesn't know I'm here, but I had to come. I can't pretend I don't want you anymore. As wrong as it is, I think about you constantly. I lay awake all night wondering what you're doing, what you are thinking. It's crazy, but I need you, Daniel. In all the ways a person needs another person. I need to feel your heart beating against my chest."

"It should be obvious from this afternoon, I want you too."

"Tonight I want you to take me all the way. I need you to pretend this ring I wear on my finger means nothing, as it does for me. Can you? Are you willing to go against what others deem wrong and give me all the love you have to give? I beg you to not think of me as another man's wife, but as the woman who would do anything to break free from her chains and be yours."

"I can. I'd do anything for you."

She stepped in closer, the wind gusting in and blowing her hair wildly.

"You must be cold. I worry you'll catch cold from our time in the rain earlier."

"To look at you warms me from the inside."

Daniel stood from the bed and felt the cool breeze against his bare chest. Tears streaked her damp face. He stared at the outline of her nipples from beneath the thin material.

"I didn't know what else to do. I've tried to stop thinking about you. The harder I try, the more I crave to be with you. When I left you today all I knew was it was right. I won't believe anything else. I won't feel shame or guilt. Everything about you is right, feels right...tastes right."

"I've been wanting you to come in here. As you are. I had a dream about it last night."

"You did? And what happened?"

"I made love to you. All night. I watched your body writhe in spasms while you screamed and called out my name. I took you all night, never letting you out of my arms for a second."

She pulled her dressing gown off over her head and tossed it to the side. The sight of her nearly sent him spinning. He drank in her beauty. Each delicious curve, her skin soft, supple, and smooth. Her nipples hypnotized him, summoning him like a slave. He wanted to reach out and touch her, to make sure she was real and not a figment of his imagination. He was still trying to grasp that he'd been with her earlier.

"I need you to be sure, Evelynn. I don't want you to wake up in the morning sorry we did this. What I need to hear is...this is right with you. To go all the way, full consummation. In your mind, body and soul. Because I don't want you to regret it. It would be the same as hurting you. And I could never live with myself if I caused you pain."

She shook her head, a wild gleam in her eye illuminated by a flash of lightning.

"No regrets. I wouldn't have come if this weren't what I wanted. My body burns for you. Do what you will with me. I assure you...I want this more than anything I've ever wanted. I had a taste of you and I want more. I *need* more."

She came up to him swiftly and wrapped her arms around his neck, bringing his head close. He could smell a mixture of sweet perfume and the evening rain. A loud rumble of thunder had her crushing against him. Her body was slick with the rain, but still hot against his flesh.

It was all he could do to keep from devouring her right there. She deserved it slow and gentle. Their first time didn't need to be rushed.

"Kiss me. I beg you."

"I'll give you anything you want," he growled, and he meant it.

She tilted her face up and brushed her nose against his.

The first contact with her lips was magnetic, even more than before. Her lips tasted of sugar and apples. Sweet apples from the orchard. He rested his hands against her lower back and felt charged. This wasn't a fantasy. He could see, taste, smell, hear, and feel her.

A faint sigh escaped her throat as she parted her lips. The smooth texture of her tongue ran alongside his. She tasted of pastry. Daniel fought the voices of reason. The ones that told him to stop and think about what he was doing. He could die if people found out. Even the fear of death couldn't stop him now. It was too late. He'd sampled the forbidden fruit and it made him ravenous for more.

Her hands traveled to his pants and she pulled them down, rustling them from around his bare feet. Clearly, he wanted her and she liked seeing it for herself. His cock pounded to be set free and wrapped in the confines of a softer, more fragrant place. To lay in her womb and let her sweetness nurture him until he showered her with his undying love.

"I want you to have me the way you dream about me."

The passionate look in her eyes was enough.

Chapter Twenty-one

She stood before him, offering all of herself in a way she'd never done before. Next door was a man who didn't know what she wanted and needed to feel like a woman. Words were lost on him. Actions were futile. But not with Daniel. Tonight signaled the end of her restless ways and shattered heart. It was healing with every look of love he bestowed on her.

Vulnerable and empowered she ran her hands along her breasts. She rolled her head to the side and gazed at him through her lashes with a wanton lust that had always been there, waiting to be unchained.

"Don't treat me as if I'm fragile. Tonight I don't want to be a lady. Breathe new life into this body as only you can."

He nodded and came at her, picking her up and kissing her breasts playfully at first, then more forcefully. Toward his bed he carried her and set her down gently.

"What are you going to do to me?"

"It will be a surprise."

He folded his handkerchief and brought it up to her eyes. "You will like what I do to you. I promise."

Evelynn moistened her lips. Excitement flowed through her veins. He kissed her on the cheek and tied the cloth around her eyes. The sudden darkness made her feel bold. She would never have dared put all her trust into another person the way she trusted him. Her heart leapt with the newness of it all.

"I'm going to touch you everywhere, taste you everywhere. You are at my mercy until I say otherwise. Any objections?"

She mouthed the words "no" but it was lodged in her throat. Instead she shook her head and he laughed.

"Good girl. I've waited for the chance to discover your body and now I'm going to enjoy it."

Evelynn felt his hot breath on her neck. The tip of his nose nuzzled close and circled around, etching imaginary words of love on her sensitive areas. His tongue flickered along her earlobe and drew down her neck, pebbling her skin with a layer of goose bumps. Her thighs quivered. The wonderment of where his hands were and what they would do next kept her sense on high alert.

He trailed his tongue down and sampled her nipples until they'd become impossibly tight, pulling at her skin and edging closer to his mouth. Where his tongue was not, his fingers were, pinching and squeezing until she squealed in delight.

He knocked her knees open and a draft rushed between her legs. Would he touch her there next? The anticipation was overwhelming.

"Turn over. I want your chest to rest on the bed with your bottom high in the air."

The order was enticing and furthered her excitement. His hands kneaded her fleshy hips and slid across her backside. He spread her flawless bottom, sending shivers everywhere. It was an eternity before she felt his tongue run along the length of her nether region, starting from her hidden nub. His tongue flickered along the tiny muscle of her clit until she could feel it throbbing. He switched between darting his tongue and lapping at her, fully extending its slick wetness deep inside her walls.

She groaned, swiveling her body left to right, allowing for him to get as far in as he could. Without warning, he stretched her wide and inserted two fingers inside her drenched channel. He held them there until she started squirming, and plummeted them into her hard and fast.

"Yes, Daniel, yes."

He pulled out his fingers and ran his tongue inside her again.

"You taste delicious. I'll never tire of drinking your juices."

His words were as powerful as his tongue and fingers, making her want every orifice of her body to be filled. There came a moment when she didn't feel anything. Where had he gone? Her core pulsated along with her heartbeat, a cadenced chant begging for something to take away her emptiness.

The sound of his voice next to her ear vibrated down to her toes, sending mouthwatering visions to her brain. "I want you, Evelynn. Can you feel how much I want you?"

She was about to answer no when she sensed him near. The length of his shaft against the back of her thigh made her whole body convulse. "What would you say if I asked you to taste me the way I tasted you? Does the thought repulse you?"

"No, not at all. I've dreamt about doing with my mouth the same things I would with my hands."

"Turn and kneel in front of me."

"On the floor?"

"Don't worry, I've put some blankets down to soften the impact on your knees."

Evelynn knelt and reached her hand forward until she felt his leg. Slowly she slid her hand up and over, grasping his thickness in her hand. It felt harder than before and instinctively she parted her lips. She'd never tasted a man there before and liked how Daniel would be her first and only. She leaned forward, his size filling the width of her mouth, the texture sleek against the roof of her mouth. The experience was new for her but she took to it immediately. Her lips wrapped around him tight and she pushed forward and pulled back, sucking him as she neared the tip.

His hands lightly held her head against him, daring her to swallow him a little more each time she took him in.

She found a steady rhythm and between her hands and mouth she consumed him greedily. It surprised her how much it stimulated her own sex by pleasuring him. She imagined him watching her take him into her mouth, her lips glazing along his cock.

"Okay, my beauty, you are far too eager."

Evelynn pulled away. "Did I do something wrong?"

"No. You almost made me burst. It's time to cater to your needs again. You looked luminous with my erection between your pink lips."

He laid her back on the bed and spread her legs to either side of him. The thought of his thick mass inside her sent her pulse racing.

"I want you to bring your legs up and bend your knees back to where they almost touch your breasts."

Evelynn bit her tongue to keep from telling him to hurry. Not only was it unladylike, but part of the delirious pain was not knowing when it was coming. He spread her a little wider and she knew how exposed she was. She struggled to keep from rolling side to side. The head of his penis prodded against her opening and moved against her thigh. He teased her on and off several times. Frustrated she let out a loud sigh.

"Please. No more teasing me. Two years I've waited for this moment. Don't make me wait another second."

"In good time. I'm savoring the moment. It shouldn't be rushed."

"I beg you. Fill me up. Love me like no other man ever has."

She waited. Poised for his initial strike. The cloth was removed from her face and she was treated to his handsome face hovering above her. "I want to see the sparkle in your eyes when I enter you."

"Yes."

He rocked her knees up to her chest even further, opening her channel wider. A noise from outside startled her and she held her breath.

"Do you think?"

"No. You are safe. It's the wind. The storm has picked up."

"Okay." She pushed back the thoughts of Brandt walking in on them and focused on the incredulous moment about to come.

He rested the tip of his sex at her opening and gently eased her inner folds apart. Inch by inch she took him in, her walls expanding, until he was fully in her cavern. Evelynn let out her breath and watched his expression. Neither of them moved or said a word, but she was sure a million thoughts were running through his mind as well. Was this a dream? Had either one ever expected to feel like this? The beat of her heart shut out the sounds of the storm as they celebrated their first union.

He pulled out a little ways and dived in again, managing to go farther still. Her body shook around him, her knees flailing around. She was vaguely aware of being in the barn, but they could have been anywhere. His gaze explored her body, his smile draped her in warmth, and his eyes reflected appreciation. This was love. Not the physical act they were partaking in, but the moment where they were entirely connected in body, mind, and soul. It was theirs to cherish forever.

"Deeper, go deeper," she heard herself say.

Daniel sped up his action and adhered to her request. Faster and deeper, filling her up wider each time. She met his movement again and again.

"I'm close. Oh God, I'm close."

They filled the quiet barn with the sound of their panting and groaning. She was aware of how close he was, and it helped her reach the point she had longed for. The explosion nearly split her body apart. He continued to pump hard, slamming into her, until she felt his climax spill inside her. His thrusts slowed and he released a low, deep moan. Daniel let her legs go and they flopped to the bed. She was spent, and was certain he was too.

He lay with her, winding the ends of her hair around his fingers. Slowly the sounds of the outside world came back and they nestled close together on the small mattress, neither wanting to part from the other.

"Did you enjoy?"

"I did. It was torture with my eyes covered. My body was on fire waiting for what you'd do next."

Daniel stroked her cheek with the back of his fingers. "You are beautiful. I've always known it, but tonight you were radiant."

A bright flash of lightning startled them as a dark figure loomed over them. The face of a monster ready to tear their eyes out flickered again followed by a tremendous crashing of thunder.

Evelynn screamed.

Chapter Twenty-two

Brandt stood over them, his face set in rage.

"I guess I am the fool after all. I tried to convince myself you two weren't out here together. As I was falling asleep I'd heard a sound, but didn't expect you would get up in the middle of the night to come lay with him. Is this how a wife honors her husband? Naked in bed with the likes of a thief and liar?"

Evelynn tried to speak, but her voice betrayed her. Fear brought a sudden chill to her body.

"What? You have nothing to say? Seems to me you had all kinds of things to say earlier. Or do you reserve your petty thoughts only for supper?"

"Brandt, I..."

Daniel was up in a flash, grabbing his trousers and pulling them on. He ran his hands through his hair and paced, mumbling quietly to himself.

She tried again to speak. Somehow she needed to find a way to explain. "If you'll only hear me out. I tried to tell you..."

"Shut up, woman! This time I will do the talking. You wonder why I don't communicate with you, it's because you make everything complicated. There can't be only one issue to deal with, there has to be a multitude of them. I don't know what more you want when I give you everything."

"What you give me are external things. They don't show me love. You refuse to listen to me."

"Silence! You asked for a house, I built one. You asked for a maid, I provided you with one. You don't wish to cook, clean, or tend to the chores, I allow it. You ask to teach Bess how to sew, I agreed. What more do you require?"

She felt tiny in the bed with his massive body towering above her. "Love. True and honest love. Without expectations. The freedom to express myself and have you listen instead of wondering what you need to give me to fix it. To listen without judgment and see me for the woman I am. You had a notion of what you expected out of a wife and I am not that person. I tried to change, but you wouldn't change."

She scanned the floor looking for her dressing gown but couldn't see it. This wasn't the scene she wanted and she felt cheated of her final minutes with Daniel.

Evelynn gripped the blanket around her and climbed out of the bed, backing toward the wall.

"Why bother to hide yourself at this point? Hmm? It would seem we've both seen you out of your clothes."

She ignored him and used her feet to find her gown. Evelynn quickly put it on, trying to keep as much of her body covered as she could. She had no idea morning had come.

"Now that you are decent, I want you to leave here this minute. We will finish this discussion when I am finished here."

"I won't. We have things to straighten out first. All three of us."

"Like hell. The damage is done. You have yourself to thank. Get in the house and get cleaned up. You look like a drowned rat."

"I won't go."

"You will or I'll toss you there myself."

The temple in his forehead throbbed violently and she backed away. Daniel stood and positioned himself between them. It was then she noticed his back and all the raised cuts and lashes.

Anger quickly replaced her fear. "What happened? How did his back get all marked up?"

She looked from her husband to Daniel and the answer became clear.

"How dare you lay a hand on this man? He's been nothing but your dutiful servant. Putting up with you day in and day out? Is this what I have to look forward to? Are you going to take out your anger the same way on me next?"

Brandt glared at her from beneath a tangle of eyebrows.

"Woman, you have forgotten your place! You don't want to know how I plan to teach you respect."

He rose as if to strike her when Daniel caught his wrist and clenched it tight in his fist.

"There will be no harm done to this woman. Ever. I will see you rot in Hell before a single hand is laid on her. Do I make myself clear?"

"Evelynn, I suggest you get into the house right now. I'll not have you telling me what to do. I am still your husband and while you're my wife, you'll do as you are told. Go now and I'll consider sparing this man's life."

"You swear?"

"The longer you stand here, the less apt I am to let him go."

It tore her up to think Daniel suffered. She wanted to reach out and embrace him, but not in front of Brandt. "I'm sorry, Daniel."

The rain still came down and the sky was a charcoal gray. She ran to the house and let the tears come. Would her husband spare the life of the man she loved? For once she would have to trust him to stay true to his word.

そ そ そ

It was still raining buckets of water and the embankment was soaked. Harris eyed the line of the water through his rain-speckled glasses, fearing the worst. It was already four feet below the top of the dam and would only continue to rise as the weather worsened. He tilted his hat up and scratched his forehead. To say he was nervous was an understatement.

Many things should have been done. He'd warned the board when they appointed him. The lining on the upper slope needed to be renovated. The people may not have wanted more money spent on the dam repairs or the piping, but he should have pushed them harder to listen to him.

This was bad, very bad. He had been certain the rain would come to an end and the reservoir would level off. The floods in the past had all been minor but this time it had the potential for disaster. People were counting on him and he'd blindly led them to a false sense of security.

As unintentional as it was, he had been wrong. It was too late to try and fix the problem, there wasn't time to man the reservoir or make any last minute changes. He wondered if the others knew this day was coming and wanted someone else to point fingers at. The blame would rest solely on his shoulders. He shook his head. What a costly mistake. Business sense he had, common sense he lacked, and he was proving it to himself.

Harris looked around to make sure no one had seen him evaluate the water level. He estimated in an hour, the entire downtown square would be flooded, not to mention any of the homes surrounding it. If he wanted to make it out unscathed, he needed to head for the hills and make his way to Virginia where he'd heard several businesses were coming into some money. To stay here would prove disastrous for his life in one way or another.

He hurried to his house to pack up as few of his belongings as he would need. Especially food and other small provisions. On his way through town he would do his best to alert the people to move to higher ground. There should have been more warning, but he'd made a gamble and lost big. All he could hope for was minimal damage and few casualties.

Chapter Twenty-three

"How did you want to settle this?" Brandt rolled up his sleeves, his muscles rippled beneath his skin.

Daniel recognized the familiar glint in his eye. There was no question the man was far stronger, he wasn't requesting proof. In fact, he was tired of fighting. It wasn't in his nature to be violent. "I don't have an answer for you. I'm sorry I didn't come straight out and tell you right from the beginning. I'm in love with Evelynn."

He didn't even bother to duck out of the way as Brandt's fist met him square in the jaw. He'd take it like a man. The pain shot up through the side of his face but he refused to give into it.

"Feel better?"

"You'll never have her. I won't lose her to you."

"She's not a piece of property. She's a person."

"And she's my wife."

"I won't steal her. She wants a chance to be loved and I can love her. For seven years she's waited for you to be the man she hoped she'd married and you let her down. Do you want her to be miserable her whole life?"

"Don't talk to me as if I don't know my own wife. These matters are between her and I. They don't include you. As of yesterday you were finished as my apprentice. I expect you to pack up what little things you brought with you and be on your way."

"Yes, sir."

"I'll not give you a penny after the crime you've committed. I could have you tried for adultery, but if you leave willingly, I will spare you the embarrassment."

Daniel shook his head. "You don't get it, do you? It's all about power and control. You can't make her love you. Hell, you can't even make her stay. She's been like a trapped bird for half her life. She can't wait to break free. If you don't let her go, she'll find a way to leave on her own."

"I'll be keeping a sharper eye on her from now on. It's none of your concern."

He rubbed his head in disappointment. "She'll go crazy being penned up. Ah forget it. I tried. I tried to warn you. If she leaves on her own accord, her life could be in danger."

"What do you mean?"

"If she left in the middle of the night, her only intent in getting away, she could wind up lost, hurt, or worse. She's led a sheltered life. She doesn't know how to defend herself. Right now she's vulnerable."

A thunderous sound caught Daniel's attention and distracted him for a split second. What the hell was that?

Harris' words about the dam went through his mind but were quickly put to rest.

Brandt pulled a knife from out of his pocket and turned it over in his hands. "I was prepared to use this. Considered cutting you while you were sleeping with my wife in your arms. I wanted her to see to what level I would go to keep her. I still am."

Chapter Twenty-four

Evelynn stormed through the house, shouting at the top of her lungs and livid with anger at herself. She'd been a stupid, stupid woman. Careless and selfish, and because of it Daniel would be the one to pay.

Bess bustled into the room and tried to offer her help. She knew the woman meant well, but she was stuck and didn't know how she was going to get out of it.

"Maybe tea will calm your stomach, ma'am. I could make you some."

"You're kind, but no, thank you. My nerves are a mess right now. I couldn't eat or drink a thing."

"It will get sorted out."

"I'm afraid this may be the calm before the storm."

"They will work it out."

Evelynn shook her head and paced some more. "They've been out there a long time. I'm afraid for Daniel."

"They are grown men and can handle themselves."

"Brandt was angrier than I've ever seen him. I can't blame him. He has every reason to be furious, catching us in each other's arms, but I don't know why he cares. It's not as though we've meant anything to one another. This marriage was never based on love. Only convenience."

"Mr. Whitling is the type of man who doesn't care to share his personal belongings. You belong to him."

"But I don't. Nor do you. Others may think so, but it's not the way I think. We are people and can't be bought or owned. I'm not like the other women in town. There has to be more. This can't be how the rest of my life goes."

Bess smoothed out her apron. "There will be more. You always tell me things will get better."

Evelynn shook her head.

"I told you not to listen to me. I'm a stupid woman! You should see Daniel. His whole back is covered in terrible looking welts and bruises. It's all my fault. I knew better. I should have resisted the urges and stayed away."

"It would take a strong woman to resist the charms of a man as handsome as Daniel."

"I did try. For two years, I've pushed him away. The moment Brandt started to suspect something I should have let it go. I ignored the warnings of my instincts. He's been slowly building into a rage and I have finally pushed him to his limit. I can't leave them in there together. I should do something."

Bess put a hand on her shoulder and patted it gently. "It's hard to walk away from love, isn't it?"

Evelynn smiled. "You're a smart woman. It is hard to walk away from love. Especially when in the end, you can't have it."

She knelt down to the floor and sobbed. Brandt thought he could keep her here, but she would leave. She'd brave the darkness of the forests and the coldest winters to find a little moment of peace. With or without his permission, she would find a way to be with Daniel.

All of a sudden a low rumble that grew to a fierce roar resounded from outside. Her blood ran cold. What on earth could make such a hideous noise?

ê ê ê

Harris watched from safety of the hill as the dam burst and sent water barreling toward the whole of Johnstown. The size of the wave was far greater than he'd feared and gained incredible speed. Impact on the foundations was horrific. Not even his worst nightmares could have prepared him for the magnitude of damage.

The water raged as it slammed against anything in its way, knocking down trees and buildings, fences and telegraph poles. Windows crashed in, signs were whipped up into the air and catapulted yards away. The sounds frightened him as much as what he was witnessing. Whole roads were lifted and merged with houses and barns. Sadly he watched his own one-story home completely crumble into bits of firewood.

The screams of the people who had nowhere else to go sent pangs of guilt throughout his body. Animals were thrust into the rushing water, never seen again. No one believed the severity of the flood warning. In horror he watched the church topple over and he said a silent prayer, in hopes of forgiveness. Before anyone saw him, he needed to leave. More than his reputation was on the line. His life was too. He would have to move, change his appearance, and most importantly, his name.

His weary legs wobbled as he walked along the loose embankment. *It should never have come to this*, he chanted to himself.

Chapter Twenty-five

Daniel kept his eyes fixed on the knife in Brandt's hand. The man had become unstable and he didn't trust him.

"Killing me won't repair your marriage. Evelynn deserves the kind of love you are incapable of giving her."

"Lies, all lies."

"You would know this if you ever took the time to listen to her wants."

"You have no idea what she wants. If you hadn't come here, we would be doing fine."

"Maybe so, but you can't change what has happened. You can only improve on it."

Brandt swiped the knife through the air. "Pack up your things and go before I use this."

"Will you let her come with me? Will you let the woman you claim to own have a chance at a happier life? Don't you want to see her smile again?"

"I'll not lose her to the likes of you. Ever."

Daniel shrugged his shoulders and reached under the bed for his walking stick. It was one of the few things he wanted to bring with him. He felt a change take place and stood back up slowly, ready for anything.

"Thought you would trick me, hey? Well I'm through being the fool."

"What?"

Brandt's answer came in the form of a sharp piercing pain in his upper shoulder. He gasped, but refused to show the intensity of the injury. The knife punctured his skin and brought a small spurt of blood down his arm.

"Thought you would surprise me with a stick against the back of my head."

Daniel fought the urge to swing it and pummel him with it. "No. It's a walking stick I carved. I planned to use it on my way to Virginia."

The sneer on Brandt's face faded and he dropped the knife to the floor. "Like Hell!"

"As always, you'll think what you want. I am tired of wasting energy on you."

Brandt's sneer deepened. "Get out of here and don't come back. You aren't welcome in Johnstown."

The doors flung open followed by an enormous wave of water. It knocked him over and sent him crashing into the far wall of the barn. He could barely hear Brandt yelling to him with all the water clogging his ears.

"What the hell is going on?"

"The dam broke. I'm sure of it."

The water continued crashing in until the wall broke free. Brandt grabbed on to him right before they got caught up in the wave and both were sent downstream.

Daniel went underwater several times and bobbed back up, gasping for air. The water was thick with mud and debris. He kept his eyes shut tight but oil clung to his eyelashes burned when he blinked. Sharp sticks and broken glass sliced at his skin, making cuts everywhere. He heard the shouts of people—some he was certain he knew, and others he'd never before seen—but was helpless to do anything. Bodies of farm animals along with whole rooftops crammed along in the water with him. His one shoulder was causing him a considerable amount of grief but he tried using it to paddle him closer to the embankment. Brandt clung on to his other arm and wouldn't let go.

Up ahead he watched a long tree come crashing down but didn't completely dislodge from its roots. He saw it as the only chance he had to get out of the treacherous current. Daniel stretched his arm out and grabbed for it, catching enough of a stray branch to haul himself in closer. He could feel the pull of the water, trying to bring him along with it.

"I've got a hold of a tree. Let go of me and grab onto the other side!"

"I'm not letting go."

More debris barreled down onto him and he listened to the screams of people who were stuck in the watery clutches.

"You have to! You're weighing me down too much. You're sapping all the energy I need to get us out. We need to hurry or the tree is going to come loose!"

"Never. If this is to be my fate, I will accept it. But I will not let you stay behind to take my Evelynn from me."

Daniel couldn't believe it. "Are you crazy? If you want to see your wife again, you need to let go of me. Now!"

Before he could convince him to let go, the tree came loose partway, and swung him further out. The force was fierce enough to send the blacksmith hurtling back out into the raging waters.

"Brandt!"

He watched his former boss try and grab hold of anything floating nearby, but the strength of the floodwaters was too much. Daniel pulled his legs up on the tree and climbed backwards until he could reach the embankment. It, too, was flooded with the water coming up to his waist. He snatched up anything he could find to help hoist himself up to higher ground where the water only came to mid-calf. He was torn on whether to go and look for Brandt or not. His anger made him think better of it, but it wasn't a time for revenge.

As he walked, he stared in awe at the level of damage the flood had produced. Harris had been right to be concerned, but where was the warning? The land around him was bare. Trees had been ripped out of the ground. It took a moment for the magnitude of the destruction to hit him. How many homes had been destroyed? He didn't even know where he was. Nothing looked familiar. His shoulder throbbed. The mixture of debris and oil irritating his wounds made him dizzy. He found a turned over wagon that hadn't been completely destroyed and climbed onto it. He only needed a little rest. He would make sure Evelynn was all right.

Chapter Twenty-six

When Evelynn opened the door to look outside, a pool of water poured in. It swirled up around her knees, nearly knocking her down. More water filtered in and she had to grab hold of the banister to get her balance.

"Mrs. Whitling!"

She could hear Bess hollering from the kitchen in panic.

"Don't worry. Gather up whatever food you can and I'll grab the candlesticks. We need to get upstairs right away!"

The windows shattered, sending glass everywhere.

"Hurry, Bess!"

Wood creaked and groaned like a thousand people trapped inside the walls. She feared what had become of Brandt and Daniel.

"Mrs. Whitling, I was able to grab a couple loaves of bread I took out of the oven only a few minutes ago."

"It will do. There isn't time to grab anything else. We need to keep going up. I fear there will be nothing left of the downstairs. Hurry, you first." Evelynn climbed the stairs behind Bess.

"You must be cold."

Evelynn looked down and realized she was still in her dressing gown. She tore open her wardrobe closet and found a thick robe. It would do.

She ran to the window and tried to flip the latch but her hands were too slippery. Between slants of heavy rain and dirt she could scarcely make anything out. What she couldn't see was the barn. A chill went up her spine and made the hairs on the back of her neck stand up. She couldn't breathe. It wasn't happening. Evelynn put her hands over her mouth and screamed.

Bess ran over and huddled into her like a frightened child. "What is it? Why did you scream?"

"I can't see the barn! I-It's gone! All gone!"

"Are you sure? How can you see out of the windows? They're covered in dirt."

"Because there'd be a dark brown blob off to the side, and there isn't."

Evelynn moved from Bess and leaned against the wall. She slid down and wrapped her arms around her knees. Tears welled in her eyes.

"I have to try and get outside. I need to know or I'll sit up here and think the worst."

"You can't. It isn't safe."

The house swayed and rocked. Pictures fell from the wall, littering the floor.

"Oh, ma'am, I'm frightened. What if we plunge to our death?"

The house buckled sharply again and the grandfather clock crashed to the floor. She grabbed for Bess, needing her company to figure out what they should do.

"I think we need to go back down."

"But the water…"

"Yes, I know, but I'm afraid we'll be crushed if we stay up here. The walls aren't sturdy."

"I don't know. I have a feeling we will be safer up here."

She studied Bess' wide eyes.

"I am sure you're right, but I have to risk it. I have to know what happened to Daniel…and Brandt. Through all the floods we've suffered, at no time has the water ever risen this high. I'm afraid of what else is out there."

"Which is why we need to stay up high, Mrs. Whitling."

Evelynn didn't know what to do. If Daniel were in danger, she needed to help him. It frightened her to think anything bad happened to him. She worried about Brandt as well. For all their problems, she did care about him. Her stomach was tied up in knots.

"I have to go, Bess. I promise to come right back. You stay here. It will help to know you are safe. Brandt built this house well and it seems to be standing firm now. You're going to be okay."

"I don't want you to go."

She hugged the woman to her breast. "I will hurry. I may not even be able to get out there. It's all a great big unknown and I think that frightens me more than anything else."

Bravely she got up and let the robe slip off. If it got wet, it would only weigh her down. Downstairs she could hear the water sloshing about from one side of the wall to the other.

As Evelynn came to the last few steps of the stairway, she was met with rising water. She never liked the water, but she didn't have a choice. It was time to face her fears. Her legs shook as she took the stairs one at a time, making sure to get a solid footing. The dining room table bobbed along with the chair from Brandt's parlor. Broken dishes and glass floated on top. The pair of moccasins Daniel had worn still hung from the top of the brass hook. She hoped that was a good sign.

Evelynn went for the next step but the floor collapsed under her feet and sent her into the cold, dirty water. She coughed and sputtered from swallowing a little.

"Don't panic." She talked herself through it, certain it couldn't be as bad as she was picturing. Her feet found the floor and she was able to stand, the water coming close to her waist. Using her hands as oars, she propelled herself forward and tried the door. It proved difficult to open and she had to tug with all her strength. When it opened, she was shocked.

Everything was gone. She gripped the doorknob to keep from being pulled out into the water. Once she got out there she would never make it. She'd never learned how to swim. Her heart sunk as she realized there wasn't anything left of the barn. It had all vanished. Nothing but mud brown. As far as her eyes could see. Everything familiar to her was underwater.

The emptiness returned, hitting her hard in her stomach. It didn't seem possible. No flood had ever done this much damage before. The house creaked and groaned again and she saw it tilt from out of the corner of her eye.

"Bess!"

The ceiling started to fall and she had a difficult time getting out of the way. She dove for the dining room table and climbed on top of it. If she could use it as a raft, she might be able to get out. The house made a horrendous crunch as it all started to come down. She heard the windows bust in and Bess scream. As the house caved in, she was able to force the table to move out the doorway, but not before a heavy board fell onto her leg. She looked back, hoping to see Bess. There wasn't any movement. An eerie quiet settled in the air and the skies started to get dark.

She rested her head on her arm and let the rocking of the water help her mind shut down. It would help ease the panic of how many people she had lost today. Including the man she considered to be the love of her life.

Chapter Twenty-seven

As the night settled in, she opened her eyes. She couldn't even see the water anymore. It was completely coated with a thick layer of sticks and debris. Afraid to move and fall off, Evelynn gripped the sides of the table and remained as still as possible. She shivered against the cold breeze. Tears had long since dried on her face, leaving her numb and distraught. She'd lost everyone.

Voices erupted from the night, faint and far away. Families who had been separated were calling to one another. Daniel was gone. Bess was gone. Brandt was gone. She thought about Mr. Jeers from the general store and his wife Linda. Had Norma been able to get her husband and five children to safety? Would she ever see Judy's smiling face again?

The quiet disturbed her. There were no crickets chirping or insects buzzing. The harshness of reality sent her stomach lurching. A fresh batch of tears released, warm streams sliding along her otherwise chilled face. She looked back and saw what was left of the houses and barns of her neighbors. Nothing but disheveled buildings, leveled to nothing but slabs of torn up wood.

Unpleasant smells and odors filled the air and left a bitter taste in her throat. A range of emotions kept going through her. Anger, sorrow, worry, pain, fear, and panic. How long would she have to wait before someone found her? She was terribly cold. There was no home to return to. No one to live for.

❧ ❧ ❧

Daniel waded through the mess and debris along the land. He looked around wildly trying to see any sign of life. It pained him how so many had been caught up in the wall of water and wouldn't see another sunrise. Silently he hoped Brandt was strong enough to make it, but he didn't think it possible. As much as he loathed the man, he didn't wish death on him. In the end, he had pitied him. He could have been a great man, with an equally great woman by his side, but he chose to ignore the things going on around him.

More bodies floated downstream. He held on to the hope that Evelynn would be found alive, safe upstairs with Bess. He was certain the foundation was high enough and Brandt swore he'd built the house strong and sturdy. Right now he needed to believe that more than anything, to rid his mind of unsettling thoughts. He had to hang onto the hope he had survived to find her and take her away from this place she considered a cage. He was tired, sore, hungry, and had lost a lot of blood from his shoulder. The oily, muddy water stung his wounds and made him want to lash out at anyone he came into contact with.

Why had there been no official warning? Harris should have realized the water level had reached dangerously high and immediately warned people. If Harris were still alive, he would mix words with him and demand to know what he had been thinking.

The walk to Evelynn became difficult and dangerous as the skies turned black. Even the moon appeared to be too frightened to come out and shine some light. He was grateful the rain had stopped. His feet dragged and felt foreign to him. Everything was foreign to him. The landmarks he had gotten to know were all gone. He didn't recognize where he was half the time, but he had to keep pushing on, staying high to the hills, and always had one eye on the water.

It was hours before he recognized where his surroundings. But the house was not standing. He looked in every direction, hoping he was wrong. He wasn't. Daniel put his hands to his mouth and called out into the night. Tears streaked his face, leaving a salty taste in his mouth.

"Evelynn!"

He walked back and forth, his whole body shaking. He could barely hold himself up.

"Evelynn!" His voice cracked as he shouted her name. "Come on, baby, I need to hear your sweet voice. Please!" He fell to his knees and looked up into the sky. It was too dark to see anything.

"Evelynn!" Her name came out in a whimper. Why wouldn't she answer him? Why was it so damn quiet? He couldn't stand it. She had to be okay. His future depended on it. She was the woman who would be his wife. All he wanted was to love and cherish her. He needed to show her all the suffering she did wasn't in vain. How he had come into her life for a reason and they had risked everything to be together. He could not go on without her.

Daniel beat his fists against his head to keep out the ugly doubts. They wanted to destroy him and make him weak. He cried into his hands. His lady was out there. He wouldn't give up searching, no matter how long it took. With everything in him, he tried one more time.

"Evelynn!"

Chapter Twenty-eight

Was her mind playing tricks on her? She thought she heard someone calling her name. Her mind drifted in and out of consciousness.

"Evelynn!"

The voice was faint, too far away to be real. It almost sounded familiar, but she knew it couldn't be. Everyone she knew was gone. It was only a matter of time before she gave in and slipped beneath the waters herself. She couldn't even feel her body anymore.

"Evelynn!"

The voice was closer now. She opened her eyes and raised her head. Her heart thudded in her chest. Breath held, she listened hard and tried to distinguish the sound from the voices she'd heard earlier of the people searching for their loved ones. She waited, but the shouting had stopped. Why did she waste her time dreaming so much? Brandt was right when he said she needed to keep her head out of the clouds and accept things for what they were.

She froze.

"Evelynn!"

There! She'd heard it with her own two ears. It wasn't a dream.

"Daniel!"

Her throat was terribly dry but she thought she'd been loud enough.

"Baby, I'm here. Can you hear me?"

"Yes, Daniel, I can hear you!"

"It's too dark. I can't make out where you are. If you keep talking to me I should be able to find you."

"I'm in the water on the dining room table."

She heard him chuckle followed by sniffling.

"I thought I lost you."

"I did too."

Evelynn could hear him moving through the water, pushing things aside. The table started to rock slightly.

"Keep talking to me, sweetheart."

"When I looked out the door and saw the barn completely gone, I gave up all hope."

"I couldn't possibly leave you without saying a proper goodbye."

He was close. Her body felt alive again.

"Evelynn." A hand brushed against her leg and she knew everything would be all right again. "You hold on. I'm going to pull you back. Hang onto the table. You don't want to be in the water. Trust me."

She held the sides as the table moved. When it stopped, she felt hands reach around her waist and grip her tight. Her body floated through the air and she was safe inside his arms. She winced as she put weight on the leg she'd injured, but she didn't want to spoil the moment.

"Your arms are like ice."

"As are yours."

He laughed. "I can't feel them."

"I can't feel mine either. But I can hear your heartbeat."

"What you hear is your heart. Mine belongs to you. I gave it to you when we first met."

"You did?"

She kissed his chest and buried her face in the crook of his neck.

"Yes. You've been keeping it safe ever since."

"I see."

Evelynn could barely make out his eyes, but she knew right where his lips were. He kissed her gingerly and held her tight against him.

"I'll never let you go again."

He stroked her tangled hair, his lips kissing at her forehead.

"I'm going to sit down on the ground. Why don't you rest your head on my leg."

"I don't think I can sleep now."

"I know. Rest your eyes. There's nothing we can do until the sky lightens. It shouldn't be too much longer."

Carefully she got to the ground, favoring her leg. She hoped it wasn't broken.

"I don't think I want to see the damage. I fear what has become of Johnstown."

"What little I was able to see would break your heart. We will leave here at first light."

"Where will we go?"

"Virginia."

"What about..."

"Brandt?"

She was thankful he had said the name for her.

"We were together until his hand slipped and he let go. The water took him downstream. I don't want to give you false hope."

"What do your instincts say?"

"He didn't make it."

She loved the way he twirled her hair around his fingers. "I'm not sure what I think."

On the outside she grieved for her husband, the way a loyal wife should, but on the inside she was numb. Brandt had become an obstacle in the way of her life, freedom, and Daniel. Now that he was gone, she had mixed feelings.

"It will come to you in time."

"When I say the words 'Brandt is dead,' I am saddened but also relieved. It makes me feel bad, but not for the right reasons."

He stroked her cheek. "As I said. It will come to you in time. You don't have to react to everything right now. We've all been through a terrible shock and ordeal. Our bodies are bound to go through all kinds of emotions."

"Bess is gone."

"I had a feeling. When I saw the house...well, I don't want to say what all I thought, but I didn't think she made it."

Her lips moved to speak but not even a squeak would emerge. He cradled her into him.

"Shh. It's going to be okay."

"I hope she didn't suffer for too long."

"I don't believe she did."

"She was such a loyal and spirited woman. Never said a bad word about anyone. Even when I went off on my tangents about Brandt, she never chimed in. She was much more than the maid who saw to the things of the house. Bess was my friend."

"She was also an incredible cook."

"Yes, indeed. I feel terrible. I promised to teach her how to sew. I promised her I would but things kept happening."

"Try not to hang onto that for long, my love. It wasn't your control. You had no way of knowing."

"I know you are right. I need to let it sink in, I think."

"Why don't you close your eyes and try to drift off? I'll wake you at first light."

Evelynn yawned and snuggled her head into his lap. "Okay," she said sleepily, and made herself relax.

Chapter Twenty-nine

"Evelynn. It's time, sweetheart."

She blinked her eyes and squinted, as the sunlight was much too bright. For a moment she'd forgotten where she was, thanks to a dream she would look forward to reliving in person. When she sat up and saw what Johnstown had been reduced to, her heart stopped in her throat.

"Oh God. I can't believe it."

Daniel stood and took her hand to help her up.

She stepped on her one leg and fell into him.

"What happened? Can you walk?"

"I-I can try. A board fell on my leg when the house was caving in."

He frowned. "Why didn't you say something before?"

"I was too excited to see you, I think."

"Hmm. I'll want to have it looked at when we get to Virginia."

"I'm sure it will be fine." She looked at his shoulder in concern. "What happened to you?"

"Long story."

Evelynn could tell by the look on his face he was done talking about it. She had a bad feeling it had to do with Brandt.

A squeaking noise interrupted them and sitting on a long, round stick was a mouse, wriggling its nose at them.

"Daniel! Do you think it's..."

She watched his face light up like a child's when Mr. Jeers handed out free suckers at the store.

"Brill. You little sneak you."

"I can't believe he survived."

"Oh, I told you. Smart little fella. In fact, I'll bet he was keeping an eye on you for me."

He held out his hand and the mouse crawled right into it. "Sorry, little guy, but we're both going hungry this morning."

Daniel reached down and picked up the stick Brill had been sitting on.

"This is sturdy enough for you to use as a walking stick. If you find it's too rough for your hand, let me know and I'll carve some of the wood away."

He wrapped his one arm around her waist to support her and handed her the stick. "We only need to walk up a little ways. I saw a cart lodged between two fallen trees. Surprisingly it's still in good shape and I can pull you in it.

Daniel kept an even pace with her, standing on her other side like a shield from the wreckage in the water. When she tried to look, he shook his head.

"It's not what you want to see this morning."

They walked a little ways in silence, Brill squeaking every once in awhile. Her leg didn't hurt too bad as she walked, it only hurt bad when she put all her weight on it. With his help, she got along.

"It should be around here somewhere."

She squinted and saw something with wheels sticking straight up. "How about over there?"

"Yes! Good eyes. Here we go. This will be perfect."

Daniel turned over the cart and helped her in. Brill ran around it excitedly.

"How will you be able to pull me in this cart with your shoulder messed up?"

"Don't you worry. It's a short distance. Once we get to the main way, we'll take a train the rest of the way to Virginia."

"What's in Virginia?"

"Old ghosts. Along with a little money I have stored away. Enough for us to start out with. I have plenty of skills I can utilize in getting a good job. The steel industry, millwork, heck, I can even do some cabinetry. I can't promise you the world right now, but if you give me a couple years, I'll hand it to you on a silver platter."

She smiled and caressed his cheek. "Your love will be all I need right now. When you say old ghosts, what do you mean?"

"Mainly my sister."

"I'd love to hear about her. Unless it's too painful."

"It is, but it will feel good to talk about her. Holly used to be a real spirited little thing. She was about four years younger than me, but real wise for her age. You could see it in her eyes. Always bubbly, energetic, and had the kindest soul."

"I bet you were a wonderful brother to her."

"I was. Wouldn't let anyone hurt her or say mean things. At school she got teased a lot. Kids said she was a dreamer, always imagining things in her head. She loved to tell stories."

"I have a feeling I would have gotten along with her well."

"Indeed."

"You don't have to go on if you don't want."

Daniel nodded. "I was worried about someone else hurting her when I should have been paying attention to what I was doing. She wanted me to build her a tree house where she could sit and gaze up at the clouds by day, the stars by night. All of the men in my family have always built things with our hands, very skilled and talented. It made me feel good that she came to me. Made our bond more special. Right away I started building it and didn't let up until I was finished. Didn't stop to eat or sleep."

"Did she like it?"

His eyes sparkled in remembrance. "She loved it. I can still hear her squeal of excitement. Sort of the way Brill does when I bring it food."

"No wonder you take such good care of it."

"I'm glad it found a good place to hide. Where was I?"

"Holly loved the house you built..."

"There wasn't much to it. The roof could open up in a way where she could look out if she wanted, but it could close when it rained. It was hard to get her down from there. I put up thick blocks along the tree trunk to make it easier for her to climb up and down, with a rope on the other side. It was raining badly, strange too as it was during a humid summer month. She'd started to climb down the wooden blocks but one fell off so she ran over to the rope. Her hands slid and she took a big tumble."

"Oh, how awful!"

"No one had heard her because we were inside getting supper ready. When I went to get her, she was drenched and shaking. I think she was in shock. Holly couldn't get up. I carried her. She howled in pain the whole way."

"Poor thing. She must have been frightened."

"She clung to me, but I could tell she was going to lose consciousness any minute. By the time I got her into the house, she had passed out. We rushed her to the doctor and he examined her right away. She'd cracked a rib and broken her leg. Not to mention she was in shock from the intensity of the pain."

"I'm sorry, Daniel. I can't imagine how hard it was for you."

"I tried to keep her spirits up like she always did to me, but nothing would make her smile. The doctor set her leg and rib. We had to wait. As the summer wore on, she laid in bed, not wanting the curtains open or anything. It was like her spirit had died. She never smiled at me the same way."

"How come?"

"I had a feeling she blamed me."

Daniel stopped a moment and brushed away a tear.

"You couldn't have known. What you did was out of love."

"I was supposed to protect her. Keep her from harm. I messed up and let her down."

"You were only a boy, and much too hard on yourself."

"I still blame myself."

"Did her leg ever get better?"

"No, it didn't. When the doctor unwrapped her leg and checked it over, he told her she'd never be able to walk on it again and absolutely no climbing. It wasn't healing properly and he was concerned about the gash in her leg. It had become infected. I started to make her a walking stick. A cane to help her get along and make it easier."

"Did it work?"

Tears rolled down and dripped off his chin. She wanted to put her arms around him and squeeze him tight.

"She didn't get a chance to use it. The doctor told her she needed to get into a better frame of mind and that it would help her in the healing process. I think she shut everything out from there on out. She wouldn't even try and get out of bed. The infection was worse than any of us knew and the doctor was busy tending to many families who had come down with pneumonia. The infection spread quickly. There wasn't any time. The next morning she had passed on."

"Oh, Daniel. I am very, very sorry."

"It's okay. I relived those feelings of helplessness and determination when I thought for a moment that I had lost you. I-I couldn't lose you too. Nothing would have stopped me from searching for you."

She wiped a tear from her eye. "I love you."

Daniel looked back at her and winked. "You ought to know how much I love you. It shouldn't be much longer now. It's your turn to talk about something from your life. What made you think Brandt was the one to marry?"

She sighed. "I was too young to know any better. I liked the fact he was much older and was making a name for himself, but at the time I didn't see the big picture. He needed to mold someone while he built his career, and I guess I needed someone to offer me a way out of my cramped life."

"Hard times?"

"We never had money. I loved my family very much, but it was crowded in the house and we went without all the time. I thought if I left, the others would have more. Food, money, clothing, everything. I believed I could learn to love him over time."

"You have a good heart."

Evelynn chuckled. "No, I was stupid. Right away I knew I had made the wrong decision. He spent all his time working and would come home tired and sore. Brandt only made time for eating, sleeping, and smoking his pipe in the parlor. Day after day, I sat at the table lonely with no one to talk to. I tried to go out and make friends with some of the other ladies, but they either snubbed me because I lived in a great big house and wore nice clothes, or I couldn't relate with them."

"Sounds lonely."

"I was thrilled when Bess came to work for us. Brandt was adamant she earn her keep and learn her place. But I saw her as a companion and latched onto her right away. Out of fear of my husband, she wouldn't get too close to me. We found a happy medium. I needed someone to listen to me. Pay attention to me. When it neared time for him to come home, I would get a terrible knot in my stomach. It made me physically ill. His presence didn't take away the loneliness, it magnified it."

"Did you ever love him?"

"No. It's almost too wicked to admit, but no. My mother had set up a silly notion in my head about what love meant to her. My father loved her and treated her well. He worked very hard, trying to support all of us kids and take care of my mother at the same time. No matter how hard he worked he still took the time to smile and to make each of us feel special. I wanted all those things. But Brandt didn't reveal those feelings to me, and I'm not too sure he had them to begin with either."

"I know he cared for you. Not in the right way, but he cared about your well being."

"I know. And I care about him too, like a friend or if he were my brother. It was a marriage out of convenience and nothing else. I pretended every day he would finally see me and appreciate me. When you came to live with us, things started to become clear."

Daniel threw his head back and laughed. "There's something you have in common. He blames me too."

"All the qualities I'd hoped to see in Brandt were in you. The smile, the conversation, the appreciative looks. I knew I wasn't imagining them. I felt comfortable when we spoke, like it was something I'd done every day of my life. I started seeing us together in a different light. As a couple. And my dreams...they were always of you."

"I hope to love you the way you want to be loved."

"You already have."

"Can you see the tracks across the way?"

Evelynn sat up and looked out across a large expanse of land. "Okay, yes, I see it."

"We should be there in a couple hours. Have you ever ridden on a train?"

"Nope. How about you?"

"No. Later tonight we'll be lying on a bed in a hotel. How does that sound?"

"Warm and cozy. And you?"

"It gives me ideas."

Chapter Thirty

Brandt dragged his body up the muddy embankment and coughed up more water. The foul stench made him gag. He was thankful the rain had let up. The sun rose and shed light to what had been a very dark night. His lungs ached. Strewn around him were bodies, debris, and fallen trees. His arms were sore from treading water for most of the night and he was colder than he'd ever been. He looked back and didn't see any sign of Daniel. Had he made it out alive? He wondered how many survivors there were, if any.

His legs shook as he stood and a deep gash in his right thigh made him cringe with each step. Keeping to the hills, he wound his way among the remains of Johnstown, heading for home. He knew Evelynn would be fine, though scared out of her wits. Few other homes had been built as well as his.

After hours of walking, he reached the plot of land he'd worked countless hours for. Hardly recognizable he tried to imagine how it could be again, but it didn't work. All of his life's work, the blood and sweat...gone. Everything was a mess. He felt a tightness in his chest when he realized there was no sign of Evelynn. There was

Ann Cory

nothing left of the house. It laid flat, pieces everywhere. He'd been smart to build his house higher up, but it hadn't been enough. He hadn't counted on a force of water to send it toppling over.

In a moment of frenzy, he ran over and started looking through the wood planks and underneath the rafters. The smell in the air was enough to make him sick. He looked around. Nothing. Anywhere. She would have had nowhere to go to stay safe. Once again he'd let her down. What kind of man was he? If she hadn't gotten to safety, she would have been thrust down the river and he wouldn't find her for days.

Beneath a rafter that was still intact, he saw something familiar. Brandt covered his mouth with his hand while he took a closer look. Relief and shock hit him at once. Brown eyes stared up at him listlessly and he realized it was Bess. If they'd been in the house together, he was sure to find Evelynn nearby.

He waded into the water and dug through everything. His hands were bloodied and torn from the wood and pieces, but he didn't care. Brandt kept on until he was satisfied she wasn't there. All he could think was how the current had sent her down the same way he did. His heart was heavy. He ignored the shouts from those he recognized. The day would be a tough one. He would look for the bodies of both Daniel and Evelynn until he was confident they were dead. If Daniel wasn't yet, he soon would be. None of this would have happened if he hadn't allowed the young man into his practice, his home, his life.

Chapter Thirty-one

For all the times Daniel had wished to leave Virginia and all his guilt behind, he was looking forward to coming back for a fresh start. Having Evelynn by his side helped boost his spirits and made him feel like he could do anything. This was one time in his life he felt like a man, with all its expectations and responsibilities. It was time to rebuild.

He nudged Evelynn and watched her open her pretty blue eyes.

"Wake up, sleepyhead. We're pulling up to the train station now."

The train whistle blew and came to a stop. Daniel grabbed her hand and led her off, helping her down the high step. Immediately they were hit with a large crowd of people and noise. His ears perked up when he heard a young man call out the news headlines concerning the Johnstown flood.

"Evelynn, come with me a minute."

He led her through the station to the corner and asked to see the paper.

"What is it?" She leaned in, trying to see over his shoulder.

"It's news about the flood. It says over two thousand people are feared dead."

"No!"

"It says the South Fork Dam finally burst, sending over twenty million tons of water crashing down on Johnstown, Pennsylvania. The floodwaters rose to over sixty feet high and struck down everything in its path. Some of the survivors were found huddled in their attics and on rooftops, while countless others were swept downstream."

Evelynn gasped. "We were lucky."

He handed the paper back to the young man and put his arms around her.

"I hope Norma from the post office and her family made it. Their home wasn't very sturdy to begin with, but I hope they find a safe place to go. I wonder if I'll ever see Judy, Mr. Jeers, or his wife Linda, again. Or Brandt."

"Time will tell. It's going to be a while before people are found. You're trembling."

"I'm cold."

"Let us get to a hotel and we'll find you something more suitable to wear."

     ∿ ∿ ∿

Evelynn snuggled close to Daniel, thrilled to be in a nice, warm bed. Everything about Johnstown was a blur. She knew the flood had been real, but parts of it were blocked from her mind. She felt bad for not making Bess come with her and for not teaching her to sew. The woman had been her friend and she would be missed. It was hard to imagine the many people who had suffered. All she could remember was the way it affected her. No one else mattered to her except Daniel. Now they lay together the same way they had before all the terrible events occurred. Brandt had stolen their peaceful repose together and it had been given back.

He leaned his head over and brushed her hair away from her face.

"I can hear those thoughts of yours churning away. What are you thinking about?"

She fidgeted with the edge of the blanket. "Is there such a thing as starting over? I mean...do people get the chance to start fresh?"

"I believe we're going to find out. Together. What I want you to know is that while I love you, I don't expect you to hide your grief or pretend you are okay when you are not. There's no need for secrets or feeling the need to bottle emotions up inside. It isn't healthy."

"It's what I know."

"We need to find ways to help you learn to trust, share, and be yourself without worry you are disappointing or hurting someone else."

"Doesn't sound easy."

"Nothing worthwhile is easy."

"It will be easier because I have you to help me."

He touched the tip of her nose gently. "I'm right by your side anytime you need me."

She nodded her head. Daniel was always understanding and gentle. Why couldn't Brandt have learned such manners? She'd be a different woman right now and would never have met the gentleman before her.

"Do you think things happen for a reason?"

"Yes, I do. Which is why I feel strongly we've been given another opportunity together."

She lay upon the bed and sighed deeply.

"Thank you. I guess the one concern I have is finding out if Brandt made it or not. I am still legally married to him."

"We'll cross that bridge when we come to it."

"I think he died for me a long time ago. I know it sounds like I'm a heartless woman, but..."

He put his finger to her lip to quiet her.

"Please don't say such things. You are the most caring, giving, loving woman I have ever met. Sometimes two people find one another and try and make a go of it, but find they weren't a right fit. You gave Brandt all the patience in the world. You cannot live your whole life with the emptiness you had."

"Emptiness. That was what I woke up each morning feeling, as if I were missing something, but I could never quite figure it out. Almost as if in the evening things were sapped from me. But all the while, I was empty."

"Or maybe you did know, but you didn't want to believe it."

Evelynn nodded. "I believe you're right."

"I hope in time your emptiness fades. I intend to fill your days with as much romance, love, and companionship as I can. Without smothering you, of course."

She laughed and ran her hand along the smooth texture of his face. "Silly man. I've been aching to be smothered. I'll welcome all of those things you mentioned with open arms."

"I think we're going to be okay."

"I hope so. Still, I believe my grief runs more for the people of Johnstown. Some of the people, while not entirely my friends, meant something to me."

"Makes sense."

"I mean, even though I didn't socialize with them, I still cared. Many were struggling with money, illness, and depression. They may not have had much, but they brought something to the town. They made it the place it was. I will miss them."

She struggled with the tears until they won out.

Daniel put his arms around her and let her sob into his shoulder.

"I've always put my faith in nature and the world around us, ever since I was a little girl, but now I feel let down."

"You can't blame something you have no control over. It will never be resolved."

Evelynn wiped at her eyes. "The world is such a cold, cruel place at times."

"Yes. Which is why we need to make sure there are plenty of warm, happy times too. Love is still around us, even when everything else in our view has crumbled and faded away."

"I think right now I need to feel that love. Honest, it's what I want."

Daniel smiled. "It would be my pleasure."

He pulled her into him and at once she felt the hardness of his cock nestled between her thighs.

"You're a beautiful man," she whispered. "I love all the places you take me."

"We have a lifetime of exploring ahead of us."

His fingers danced around her nipples and swept them up until they needed nourishment from his lips.

"Mm. I think you've melted away the last of the ice around my heart."

"Good. Because now I'm going to try and make it race."

Daniel edged his fingers down her belly, resting for a moment as if in question. She answered by spreading her thighs. "It already is racing."

The Bounty
(c)2006 Beth Williamson

What happens when a bounty hunter finds his prey only to discover she's his mate?

A sexy hot western historical, book one in the Malloy Family series, available now in digital formats and coming in paperback July 2006 from Samhain Publishing.

Tyler raised his head from the cool water and shook his head, spraying droplets of water all over his shirt. He ran his fingers through his wet hair, wringing the moisture from it. He was surprised Nicky wasn't bellowing to be let loose. Maybe she needed to dunk her head, too. He shivered from the memory of her wet hair after her bath last night.

"Enough."

It was time to think with his brain again instead of his nether regions. This woman was still a wanted outlaw, regardless if he was in love with her. Never once did he ever feel remorse for the outlaws he dragged back for a bounty. Why the hell did he ever take Owen Hoffman's offer? He didn't know how to control his rampaging emotions, because he hadn't let himself have any for twenty years. He felt like he was pulling and yanking on that invisible thread, trying to stretch it back out between them. Like a wolf gnawing on his leg to free himself from a trap.

He filled both canteens and stomped back to the horses. At first he couldn't believe his eyes. Only his gelding Sable stood there, whinnying softly. He blinked, trying to comprehend what he saw. The shackles sat atop his saddle. She was gone.

Nicky was gone.

She couldn't have more than a few minutes head start. He jammed the shackles into his saddlebag, swung the canteens onto the saddle horn, and threw himself into the saddle.

He spurred his horse forward, glad to have such a large, fast beast. *Damn her.* How did she get free? He felt angry, betrayed, and somehow...hurt. *No.* No woman was going to turn him into a simpering fool. It was the goddamn frigging bounty that mattered, not Nicky.

He could see the fresh hoofprints in the damp, scrubby ground. The fog was making it impossible to hear anything, though. He cursed himself up and down for letting her out of his sight. No prisoner had ever escaped from him before, but then again, Nicky was no ordinary prisoner. She was his wife, his lover, his heart, his soul.

And she had just left him. And taken every scrap of warmth with her.

ȣ ȣ ȣ

Nicky hunkered down as low as she could in the saddle. The cold wind whistled through her ears as she fled from the man she loved. She had to smash her hat down on her head to keep it from flying off as her curls flapped like a flag. Her heart was trip-hammering in fear and elation. She had done it. Escaped from Tyler. She ignored the sadness that threatened to tear her heart from her chest...she'd deal with those emotions later.

She was headed east toward Nebraska, or so she thought anyway. This darned fog gave her no help. Suddenly Juliet's hooves were silent. It took a moment for Nicky to realize that the ground was gone and they were flying over the edge of a precipice. The ground rushed up at them with dizzying speed. Nicky let out a short scream before they landed, and then all was black.

ॐ ॐ ॐ

Tyler thought he'd heard something, but couldn't pinpoint the noise. As he approached the ravine that marked the border between Wyoming and Nebraska, he pulled Sable to a halt. He needed to determine which way she would go. East, definitely not west. That would lead her back toward him. He turned his horse and started to spur him forward when he saw hoofprints on the ground in front of him, facing the ravine.

"What the hell?"

She couldn't have jumped it. It was twenty feet wide at this point. Still...he dismounted with a curse. If she had, there was no way he'd catch her today. Sable couldn't make that kind of jump. He knelt to examine the tracks when his eye caught something in the ravine.

Nicky.

Oh, Jesus.

Cold, raw fear coiled in his stomach.

He picketed Sable quickly since there were no trees close by to tether his reins, then tied a rope to his horse's saddle with trembling fingers. He clambered down the side of the ravine and saw her sprawled flat on her back, arms and legs every which way, deathly still. Her horse was near death; the poor thing had two broken legs, and was wheezing slowly.

He forced his legs to move to Nicky. There was blood on her forehead and her lip was split. He could see her left arm was twisted at an unnatural angle. He knelt down on the damp sandy ground, and slowly lowered his ear to her chest.

Please God, don't take her from me.